MISTRESS OF THE RED DEATH

"Is this your work, girl?"

"Aye. It was a debt I had to pay."

"Nails of the Devil!" he swore. "A true swords-woman is worth a score of men. Will you ride with me?"

"As a companion-in-arms," I said. "I am mistress to none."

He laughed, then grimaced at my dripping sword and the fresh-split corpses that littered the floor; then swore:

"None save Death!"

SWORD WOMAN

by Robert E. Howard
immortal creator of *CONAN*

Berkley Books by Robert E. Howard

ALMURIC
BLACK CANAAN
CONAN: THE HOUR OF THE DRAGON
CONAN: THE PEOPLE OF THE BLACK CIRCLE
CONAN: RED NAILS
THE LOST VALLEY OF ISKANDER
MARCHERS OF VALHALLA
SKULL-FACE
SON OF THE WHITE WOLF
SWORDS OF SHAHRAZAR
SWORD WOMAN

ROBERT E. HOWARD
SWORD WOMAN

A BERKLEY BOOK
published by
BERKLEY PUBLISHING CORPORATION

SWORD WOMAN

A Berkley Book / published by arrangement with
Glenn Lord

PRINTING HISTORY
Zebra Books edition published 1977
Berkley edition / December 1979

ISBN: 0-425-04445-9

A BERKLEY BOOK® TM 757,375

PRINTED IN THE UNITED STATES OF AMERICA

CONTENTS

Introduction   1
    by Leigh Brackett

Sword Woman   7

Blades for France   59

Mistress of Death   91
    (with Gerald W. Page)

The King's Service   115

The Shadow of the Hun   143

INTRODUCTION

IT'S TOO BAD that Robert E. Howard didn't write more stories about his Sword Woman, Dark Agnes de Chastillon. She was quite a character . . . more intelligent than Conan, more attractive than Solomon Kane, and as fine a swashbuckler as any of Howard's heroes. Perhaps she came a little before her time. Women who could do things were not very popular in fiction back in the thirties, particularly in the adventure story field. C.L. Moore's Jirel of Joiry, who gained considerable fame at that time, operated solely in the fantasy field, where there was a good bit more latitude. It is interesting to speculate, in view of the third of the Dark Agnes stories, *Mistress of Death*, whether Howard was making a deliberate attempt to switch his heroine into that field. If so, he died before the story was finished. It was completed by Gerald W. Page, and there were no more.

It is also interesting to speculate on whether or not Dark Agnes was inspired by the Lady of Joiry. Certainly Howard was aware of Jirel. He had read *Black God's Shadow* and liked it, and said so, and he had sent a copy of *Sword Woman* lo C.L. Moore to read, (She loved it, and hoped there would be more.) But at this late date it is impossible to say which character was first conceived, or whether indeed there was any connection between them at all. (Jirel, of course, appeared in *Weird Tales* before *Sword Woman* was written.) It is reasonable to assume that Howard and Moore both got the inspiration for their martial ladies from the same sources...the historical accounts of those women to whom Howard dedicated his chronicle of Dark Agnes, from the ballad about Mary Ambree, and quite likely from that famous saint-in-armor, Joan of Arc, though saintliness is not, fortunately, a quality possessed by either heroine.

In any case, the resemblance between Agnes and Jirel is purely superficial. They both had red hair. They both wore armor and wielded swords with deadly effect. But Jirel was fire and ice, she was silken and subtle, and she dwelt in the Neverlands of fantasy, in a different continuum from Howard's historical France. Jirel was concerned with dark gods and sorcerers, with love and magic. We never really know why or how she came to be a swordwoman. She is simply the Lady of Joiry, mailed and proud and beautiful.

Agnes, on the other hand, is a total pragmatist. Howard's talents were multi-faceted, but subtle he was not, nor silken, and his heroine isn't either. Agnes lived in a hard cruel time when women were somewhat less valuable and less well-treated than the family beast of burden, which would cost money to replace. (If there was no beast of burden, she was it.) Agnes was peasant-born, to a brutal father, in a pigsty village, and she grew up tough because if she had not been tough she would not have grown up at all.

Jirel was born on the right side of a noble blanket. Agnes' claim to noble blood came from the left hand and brought her no emoluments. In *Sword Woman* we get a blow-by-blow account of how she came to take up a man's life, and if Howard's description of her betrothal and wedding day seems a little strong, that is only because the gentle ladies who more commonly figure in historical fiction were sold off to the highest bidder with somewhat more *politesse*. The custom of the arranged marriage lasted right down through the Victorian age, and it was surrounded by all sorts of nice euphemisms, but the fact remained that a man's daughter was a saleable commodity, to be auctioned for the best price she could fetch.

Agnes had the guts to make a decisive exit from an unendurable situation, and—quite literally—makes absorbing reading, and not by any means for women's libbers only. Agnes is a forthright, honest, unselfpitying, likable human being, and she has you in her corner from Page One. She has that quality which transcends sex, since it is found as often in little girls as in large men . . . the quality of courage. And her defiance of Guiscard de Clisson, when he attempts to relegate her to her "proper place," is as eloquent a statement of individual pride and self-respect as you are likely to read anywhere.

Etienne Villiers, who in his own peculiar fashion helps Agnes on her way, is a complex rogue and extremely well-drawn. The relationship that develops between him and Agnes, through betrayal, revenge, obligation, and finally, grudging respect to friendship, is fascinating in its twists and turns.

Howard was a past master at keeping a story moving full speed ahead without losing sight of characters or atmosphere. *Blades For France* is a fine rushing swinging adventure, with Agnes now well-established in her chosen world. The plot is perhaps not quite so perfectly turned as in *Sword Woman*, which has a marvelous unity, but that will not lessen the enjoyment of the story.

Mistress of Death has a different feel, a different texture. Where the other two stories are open, full of wind and sky, forests and wild rides, *Mistress* is closed in, almost claustrophobic. Action occurs in narrow alleys by night, inside inns and houses, in secret passages and cellars. In place of Etienne Villiers, Agnes finds a new comrade in the exiled Scot, John Stuart. The adventure becomes sheer grisly fantasy, in which Agnes meets and conquers an adversary far worse than the mere cutthroats who have tried to spit her on their blades. A nice relationship develops between her and Stuart, and one wishes that the series did not end here.

One more point, for the benefit of any MCP's who may happen to read these stories and say, Oh, well, they're good yarns and all that, but no *woman* could really be physically capable of doing these things.

Rubbish, my good sirs.

There is an old adage that a good big man can always take a good little man. But between those absolutes there are all shadings of size, strength, and ability. The welterweights seem to make up the bulk of the population, but men and women, and two World Wars, coupled with the opening up of new fields of endeavor, have proved beyond question that a healthy woman is physically capable of doing just about anything she wants to.

The accepted notion of the weak and helpless female has social rather than factual origins. Soft, submissive, uncompetitive women sold better in the marriage market. In addition, to be genteelly frail was a status symbol; it meant that you didn't have to work. So the eager, energetic little girl, running free as a barefoot colt, was curbed young by her mother and grandmother and aunties and nannies ... Don't be a tomboy, act like a little lady, for shame! And before she knew it she was harnessed up in women's attire, all of it designed to hamper and bind ... shoes that forced a mincing gait, petticoats and heavy skirts, corsets, stays, fathingales, bustles, tight bodices, strangling collars. Look at the Valasquez portrait of the little Infanta of Spain. Look at her waist, and try to imagine where her insides have got to. No wonder so many women died young. No wonder they were not very active. If woman's clothing down through the centuries had been part of a deliberate plot to insure her continued physical inferiority, they could not have been better designed.

Women have got rid of all that nonsense now, thank heaven ... though one does wonder why so many girls seem to have adopted Tony Lumpkin as the person they would most like to resemble. The stigma is slowly being lifted from athletics, so that hopefully the girl who is naturally good at sports and enjoys them will no longer have to choose between giving them up or being thought unfeminine. (Just as boys who are not good at sports and don't like them are considered unmasculine.)

Queen Boudicca led her armies to battle. The white armed German women fought alongside their men and frightened the wits out of the Roman legionaries. The Vikings had their shield-maidens. And even after the advent of Christianity, exceptional women continued to break out of the trap. They have served honorably as soldiers in many wars, less honorably as pirates and freebooters, but they were all good women of their hands with sword and pistol. The women who helped to open up the far places of the world were not made of custard. They could shoot a rifle and hit what they aimed at. They could withstand heat and cold, hunger, thirst, and the ever-present threat of death quite as well as their husbands.

Never underestimate the power of a woman. In one week, a year or two ago, in separate ascents, two tiny Japanese women, each weighing less than a hundred pounds, conquered Everest. There may even be women in the world who can clean-and-jerk 360 pounds of barbell, though so far only men seem to be stupid enough to want to.

In short, we know that Agnes would have been capable of doing all the things she did because living women have done them.

In addition to the Sword Woman stories, as a lagniappe, this volume includes another of those lovely fragments that Howard left behind ... the beginning of a novel, *The King's Service*, about exotic times and places that leaves one wishing, again, that it might have been completed. Ancient India, Vikings, Celts, Greeks, the wreckage of empire ... all the elements are here.

Howard had a great love for all that was lost and strange and faraway. One thinks of him sitting at his typewriter in Cross Plains, Texas, a young man dreaming great dreams of gods and heroes far beyond the narrow boundaries of his own space and time, roaming free across the wonderful landscapes he saw in his mind.

It is sad that the dreams had to come to an end so soon. But we can be glad that he left so many of them to share with us.

Leigh Bracket
Lancaster, California
December 1976

SWORD WOMAN

1

Res Adventura

"Agnes! You red-haired spawn of the devil, where are you?" It was my father calling me, after his usual fashion. I raked my sweat-dampened hair out of my eyes and heaved the bundle of fagots back on my shoulder. Little of rest was there in my life.

My father parted the bushes and called into the glade—a tall man, gaunt and bitter, darkened with the suns of many campaigns, marked with scars gotten in the service of greedy kings and avaricious dukes. He scowled at me, and faith, I would hardly have recognized him had he worn another expression.

"What are you about?" he snarled.

"You sent me into the forest for wood," I answered sullenly.

"Did I bid you begone a whole day?" he roared, aiming a slap at my head which I avoided with a skill born of much practise. "Have you forgot this is your wedding day?"

At that my fingers went limp and the cord slipped through them, so the bundle of fagots tumbled to the ground and burst apart. The gold went out of the sunlight, and the joy from the trilling of the birds.

"I had forgot," I whispered, from lips suddenly dry.

"Well, take up your sticks and come along," he scowled. "The sun heels westward. Ungrateful wench—accursed jade!—that your father should be forced to drag his old bones through the forest to bring you to your husband."

"Husband!" I muttered. "Francois! Hoofs of the devil!"

"Will you swear, wench?" snarled my father. "Must I lesson you again? Will you flout the man I have chosen for you? Francois is as fine a young man as you can find in all Normandy."

"A fat pig" I muttered; "a very munching, guzzling, nuzzling swine!"

"Be silent!" he yelled. "He will be a prop to my old age. I cannot much longer guide the plough handles. My old wounds pain me. You sister Ysabel's husband is a dog; he will give me no aid. Francois will be different. He will tame you, I warrant me. He will not humor you, as have I. You will eat stick from his hand, my fine lady."

At that a red mist waved across my sight. It was ever thus at such talk of taming. I dashed down the fagots I had mechanically taken up, and all the fire in my blood rushed to my lips.

"May he rot in hell, and you with him!" I shrieked. "I'll *not* wed him. Beat me—kill me! Use me as you wish! But I'll never share Francois' bed!"

At that hell flamed into my father's eyes, so that I should have trembled but for the madness that gripped me. I saw mirrored there all the fury and violence and passion that had been his when he looted and murdered and raped as a Free Companion. With a wordless roar he lunged for me and dealt a buffet at my head with his right fist. I avoided the blow, and he smote with his left. Again his fist flailed empty air as I dodged, and then with a cry like the yell of a wolf, he caught my loose hair in his fingers, wrapping the tresses around his hand and wrenching my head back until it seemed my neck would break; and he smote me on the chin with his clubbed right fist, so that the sunlight went out in a wave of blackness.

I must have been senseless for some time—long enough for my father to drag me through the forest and into the village by the hair of my head. Regaining consciousness after a beating was no new experience, but I was sick and weak and dizzy, and my limbs ached from the rough ground over which he had dragged me. I was lying in our wretched hut, and when I staggered up into a sitting position, I found that my plain woolen tunic had been taken from me, and that I was decked in wedding finery. By Saint Denis, the feel of it was more loathsome than the slimy touch of a serpent, and a quick panic assailed me, so I would have torn it from me; but then a giddiness and a sickness overcame me, and I sank back with a groan. And blackness deeper than that of a bruised brain sank over me, in which I saw myself caught in a trap in which I struggled in vain. All strength flowed out of me, and I would have wept if I could. But I never could weep; and now I was too crushed to curse, and I lay staring dumbly at the rat-gnawed beams of the hut.

Then I was aware that some one had entered the room. From without sounded a noise of talking and laughter, as the people gathered. The one who had come into the hut was my sister Ysabel, bearing her youngest child on her hip. She looked down at me, and I noted how bent and stooped she was, and how gnarled from toil her hands, and how lined her features from weariness and pain. The holiday garments she wore seemed to bring these things out; I had not noticed them when she wore her usual peasant woman's attire.

"They make ready for the wedding, Agnes," she said, in her hesitant way. I did not reply. She set down the baby and knelt beside me, looking into my face with a strange wistfulness.

"You are young and strong and fresh, Agnes," she said, yet as though she spake more to herself than to me. "Almost beautiful in your wedding finery. Are you not happy?"

I closed my eyes wearily.

"You should laugh and be gay," she sighed—it seemed she moaned, rather. "'Tis but once in a girl's life. You do not love Francois. But I did not love Guillaume. Life is a hard thing for a woman. Your tall supple body will grow bent like mine, and broken with child-bearing; your hands will become twisted—and your mind will grow strange and grey—with the toil and the weariness—and the everlasting face of a man you hate—"

At that I opened my eyes and stared up at her.

"I am but a few years older than you, Agnes," she murmured. "Yet look at me. Would you become as I?"

"What can a girl do?" I asked helplessly.

Her eyes burned into mine with a shadow of the fierceness I had so often seen smolder in the eyes of our father.

"One thing!" she whispered. "The only thing a woman can do, to free herself. Do not cling by your fingers to life, to become as our mother, and as your sister; do not live to become as me. Go while you are strong and supple and handsome. Here!"

She bent quickly, pressed something into my hand,

then snatched up the child and was gone. And I lay staring fixedly at the slim-bladed dagger in my hand.

I stared up at the dingy rafters, and I knew her meaning. But as I lay there with my fingers curled about the slender hilt, strange new thoughts flooded my mind. The touch of that hilt sent a tingling through the veins of my arm; a strange sense of familiarity, as if its feel started a dim train of associations I could not understand but somehow felt. Never had I fingered a weapon before, or any edged thing more than a woodman's axe or a cabbage knife. This slim lethal thing shimmering in my hand seemed somehow like an old friend come home again.

Outside the door voices rose and feet shuffled, and I quickly slipped the dagger into my bosom. The door opened and fingers caught at the jamb, and faces leered at me. I saw my mother, stolid, colorless, a work animal with the emotions of a work animal, and over her shoulder, my sister. And I saw sudden disappointment and a haunting sorrow flood her expression as she saw me still alive; and she turned away.

But the others flooded into the hut and dragged me from the bunk, laughing and shouting in their peasant hilarity. Whether they put down my reluctance to virginal shyness, or knew my hatred for Francois, mattered little. My father's iron grasp was on one wrist, and some great mare of a loud-mouthed woman had my other wrist, and so they dragged me forth from the hut into a ring of shouting, laughing folk, who were already more than half drunk, men and women. Their rude jests and obscene comments fell on heedless ears. I was fighting like a wild thing, blind and reasonless, and it took all the strength of my captors to drag me along. I heard my father cursing me under his breath, and he twisted my wrist till it was like to break, but all he got out of me was a panting oath that consigned his soul to the hell it deserved.

I saw the priest coming forward, a wizened, blinking old fool, whom I hated as I hated them all. And Francois was coming to meet me—Francois, in new jerkin and breeches, with a chain of flowers about his fat red neck, and the smirk on his thick distended lips that made my flesh crawl. There he stood, grinning like a mindless ape, yet with vindictive triumph and lustful meaning in his little pig eyes.

At the sight of him I ceased my struggles like one struck motionless, and my captors released me and drew back; and so I stood facing him for an instant, almost crouching, glaring unspeaking. "Kiss her, lad!" bellowed some drunken lout; and then as a taut spring snaps, I jerked the dagger from my bosom and sprang at Francois. My act was too quick for those slow-witted clowns even to comprehend, much less prevent. My dagger was sheathed in his pig's heart before he realized I had struck, and I yelped with mad glee to see the stupid expression of incredulous surprise and pain flood his red countenance, as I tore the dagger free and he fell, gurgling like a stuck pig, and spouting blood between his clawing fingers—to which clung petals from his bridal chain.

What has taken long to tell needed but an instant to transpire. I leapt, struck, tore away and fled, all in an instant. My father, the soldier, quicker in wit and action than the others, yelled and sprang to catch me, but his groping hands closed on empty air. I shot through the startled crowd and into the forest, and as I gained the trees, my father caught up a bow and let fly at me. I shrank aside and the arrow thudded venomously into a tree.

"Drunken fool!" I cried, with a shriek of wild laughter. "You are in your dotage, to miss such a mark!"

"Come back, you slut!" he roared, mad with passion.

"To the fires of hell with you," I retorted; "and may the devil feast upon your black heart!" And that was my farewell to my father, as I turned and fled through the forest.

How far I fled I do not know. Behind me I heard the howls of the villagers, and their stumbling and blundering pursuit. Then only the yells, and those distant and far away, and then even they faded out. For few of my brave villagers had stomach to follow me into the deep woods, where the shadows were already stealing. I ran until my breath was jerked out of me in racking gasps, and my knees buckled, hurling me headlong in the soft leaf-carpeted loam, where I lay in a half-faint, until the moon climbed up, sheathing the higher branches in frosty silver, and cutting out the shadows yet more blackly. About me I heard rustlings and movements that betokened beasts, and perchance worse—werewolves and goblins and vampires, for all I knew. Yet I was not afraid. I had slept in the forest ere now, when night caught me far from the village with a load of fagots, or my father in his drink had driven me forth from the hut.

I rose and went on through the moonlight and the darkness, taking scant heed of the direction, so I put as much distance as possible between me and the village. In the darkness before dawn sleep overcame me, and throwing myself on the loam, I fell into deep slumber, careless of whether beast or ghoul devoured me before day broke.

But when dawn rose over the forest, it found me alive and whole, and possessed of a ravenous hunger. I sat up, wondering for an instant at the strangeness of it all, then sight of my torn wedding robes and the blood-crusted dagger in my girdle brought it all back. And I laughed again as I remembered Francois' expression as he fell, and a wild surge of freedom flooded me, so I felt like dancing and singing like a mad woman. But instead I cleansed the dagger on some fresh leaves, and putting it again in my girdle, I went toward the rising sun.

Presently I came upon a road which wound through the forest and was glad of it, because my wedding shoes, being shoddy things, were mostly worn out. I was accustomed to going barefoot, but even so, the briars and twigs of the forest hurt my feet.

The sun was not well up, when, coming to a curve in the road, which indeed was little more than a forest trail, I heard the sound of horse's hoofs. Instinct told me to hide in the bushes. But another instinct checked me. I searched my soul for fear and found it not. So I was standing in the middle of the path, unmoving, my dagger in my hand, when the horseman came around the bend, and pulled up short with a startled oath.

He stared at me and I gave back his glance, unspeaking. He was handsome in a dark way, somewhat above medium height, and rather slender. His horse was a fine black stallion, with trappings of red leather and bright metal, and he himself was clad in silk hosen and velvet doublet, somewhat shabby, with a scarlet cloak flung about him, and a feather in his cap. He wore no baldric, but a sword hung at his girdle in a worn leather sheath.

"By Saint Denis!" he exclaimed; "what sprite of the forest, or goddess of dawn are you, girl?"

"Who are you to ask?" I demanded, finding myself neither fearful nor overly timid.

"Why, I am Etienne Villiers, once of Aquitaine," he answered, and an instant later bit his lip and shook his head as if in irritation that he had so spoken. He looked at me, then, from crown to slippers and back, and laughed.

"Out of what mad tale did you step?" he asked. "A red-haired girl in tattered wedding finery, dagger in hand, in the green woodlands just at sunrise! 'Tis better than a romaunt! Come, good wench, tell me the jest."

"Here is no jest," I muttered sullenly.

"But who are you?" he persisted.

"My name is Agnes de Chastillon," I answered.

He laughed and slapped his thigh.

"A noble lady in disguise!" he mocked. "Saint Ives, the tale grows more spicy! From what shaded bower in what giant-guarded castle have you escaped, in these trappings of a peasant, my lady?" And he doffed his chaperon in a sweeping bow.

"I have as much right to the name as many who wear high-bellied titles," I answered, angered. "My father was the bastard son of a peasant woman and the Duc de Chastillon. He has ever used the name, and his daughters after him. If you like not my name go your way. I have not asked you to stop and mock me."

"Nay, I did not mean to mock you," he protested, his gaze running up and down my figure avidly. "By Saint Trignan, you fit a high and noble name better than many high born ladies I have seen simpering and languishing under it. Zeus and Apollo, but you are a tall lithe wench—a Norman peach, on my honor! I would be your friend; tell me why you are alone in the forest at this hour, with tattered wedding gown and worn shoes."

He swung suplly down from the tall horse, and stood cap in hand before me. His lips were not smiling now, and his dark eyes did not mock me, though meseemed they glowed with an inward vagrant fire. His words suddenly brought home to me how alone and helpless I was, with nowhere to turn. Perchance it was natural that I should unburden myself to this first friendly stranger—besides Etienne Villiers had a manner about him which induced women to trust him—

"I fled last night from the village of La Fere," I said.

"They wished to wed me to a man I hated."

"And you spent the night alone in the forest?"

"Why not?"

He shook his head as if he found it difficult of belief.

"But what will you do now?" he asked. "Have you friends near by?"

"I have no friends," I answered. "I will go on until I die of starvation or something else befalls me."

He mused awhile, tugging at his clean-shaven chin with thumb and forefinger. Thrice he lifted his head and swept his gaze over me, and once I thought I saw a darkling shadow pass over his features, making him for an instant appear almost like another man. Then he raised his head and spoke: "You are too handsome a girl to perish in the woods or be carried off by outlaws. If you will, I will take you to Chartres, where you can obtain employ as a serving wench and earn your keep. You can work?"

"No man in La Fere can do more," I answered.

"By Saint Ives, I believe it," he said, with an admiring shake of his head. "There is something almost pagan about you, with your height and suppleness. Come, will you trust me?"

"I would not cause you trouble," I answered. "Men from La Fere will be following me."

"Tush!" quoth he in scorn. "Who ever heard of a peasant going further than a league from his village? You are safe enough."

"Not from my father," I answered grimly. "He is no mere peasant. He has been a soldier. He will follow me far, and kill me when he finds me."

"In that case," muttered Etienne, "we must find a way to befool him. Ha! I have it! I mind me less than a mile back I passed a youth whose garments should fit you. Bide ye here until I return. We'll make a boy of you!"

So saying he wheeled and thundered off, and I watched him, wondering if I should see him again, or if he but made sport of me. I waited, and the hoofs faded away in the distance. Silence reigned over the green wood, and I was aware of a fierce and gnawing hunger. Then, after what seemed an infinite time, again the hoofs beat through the forest, and Etienne Villiers galloped up, laughing gaily, and waving a bundle of clothes.

"Did you slay him?" I asked.

"Not I!" laughed Etienne. "I but sent him blubbering on his way naked as Adam. Here, wench, go into yonder copse and don these garments hastily. We must be on our way, and it is many a league to Chartres. Cast your maiden's clothing out to me, and I will take them and leave them on the banks of that stream which turns through the forest a short way off. Mayhap they will be found, and men think you drowned."

He was back before I had finished putting on the strange garments, and chatting to me through the screening bushes.

"Your revered father will be searching for a maid," he laughed. "Not for a boy. When he asks the peasants if they have seen a tall red-haired wench, they will shake their bullet heads. Ha! ha! ha! 'Tis a good jest on the old villain."

Presently I came forth from the bushes, and he stared hard at me where I stood in shirt, breeches and cap. The garments felt strange to me, but gave me a freedom I had never experienced in petticoats.

"Zeus!" he muttered. "'Tis less perfect disguise than I had hoped for. The blindest clod in the fields could tell 'twas no man those garments hid. Here; let me lop those red locks with my dagger; mayhap that will aid."

But when he had cut my hair into a square mane that

fell short of my shoulders, he shrugged his own shoulders.

"Even so you are all woman," quoth he. "Yet perchance a stranger, passed hastily on the road, would be befooled. Yet we must chance it."

"Why do you concern yourself over me?" I asked curiously; for I was unused to kindness.

"Why, by God," quoth he, "would any man worthy of the name leave a young girl to wonder and starve in the forest? My purse holds more copper than silver, and my velvet is worn, but Etienne Villiers holds his honor as high as any belted knight or castled baron; and never shall weakness suffer while his purse hold a coin or his scabbard a sword."

Hearing these words I felt humble and strangely ashamed; for I was unlearned and untaught, and had no words to speak the gratitude I felt. I stumbled and stammered, and he smiled and gently chided me to silence, saying that he needed not thanks, for goodness carried its own reward.

Then he mounted and gave me a hand. I swung up behind him, and we thundered off down the road, I holding to his girdle, and half enveloped by his cloak which blew out behind him in the morning breeze. And I felt sure that any one seeing us thundering by, would swear it was a young man and a lad, instead of a man and a girl.

My hunger mounted with the sun, but the sensation was no uncommon one in my life, so I made no complaint. We were travelling in a south eastward direction, and it seemed to me that as we progressed a strange nervousness made itself evident in Etienne. He spoke little, and kept to the less traveled roads, frequently following bridle-paths or wood-cutters' trails that wound in and out among the trees. We met few folk, and they only yokels with axe on shoulder or fagots on back, who gaped at us, and doffed their ragged caps.

Midday was nigh when he halted at a tavern—a woodland inn, lonely and isolated, the sign of which was poorly done, and almost obliterated; but Etienne called it the Knaves' Fingers. The host came forth, a stooped, hulking lout, with a twisted leer, wiping his hands on his greasy leather apron, and bobbing his bullet head.

"We desire food and lodging," said Etienne loudly. "I am Gerard de Bretagne, of Montauban, and this my young brother. We have been to Caen, and are travelling to Tours. Tend my horse and set a roasted capon on the table, host."

The host bobbed and mumbled, and took the stallion's rein. But he lingered as Etienne lifted me off, for I was stiff from the long ride, and I did not believe my disguise was as complete as I had hoped. For the long glance mine host cast at me was not such as a man gives a lad.

As we entered the tavern, we saw only one man seated on a settle and guzzling wine from a leather jack—a fat, gross man, his belly bulging over his leather belt. He looked up as we entered, started and opened his mouth as if to speak. Etienne did not speak but looked full at him, and I saw or felt a quick spark of understanding pass between them. The fat man returned to his wine jack in silence, and Etienne and I made our way to the board on which a slatternly serving wench placed the capon ordered, pease, trenchoirs of bread, a great vessel of Caen tripe, and two flagons of wine.

I fell to avidly, with my dagger, but Etienne ate little. He toyed with his food, his gaze shifting from the fat man on the settle, who now seemed to sleep, back to me, and then out the dingy windows with their diamond shaped panes, or even up to the heavy smoke-stained beams. But he drank much, refilling his flagon again and again, and finally asked me why I did not touch mine.

"I have been too busy eating to drink," I admitted, and took it up uncertainly, for I had never tasted wine before. All the liquor which ever found its way into our miserable hut, my father had guzzled himself. I emptied the flagon as I had seen him do, and choked and strangled, but found the tang pleasing to my palate.

Etienne swore under his breath.

"By Saint Michele, in all my life I never saw a woman drain a flagon like that! You will be drunk, girl,"

"You forget I am a girl no longer," I reproved in the same low tone. "Shall we ride on?"

He shook his head.

"We will remain here until morning. You must be weary and in need of rest,"

"My limbs are stiff because I am not used to riding," I answered. "But I am not tired."

"Never the less," he said with a touch of impatience, "we shall rest here until tomorrow. I think it will be safe enough."

"As you wish," I replied. "I am utterly in your hands, and wish to do only as you bid in all things."

'Well and good," he said; "naught becomes a young girl like cheerful obedience." Lifting his voice he called to the host who was returned from the stables, and hovered in the back ground. "Host, my brother is weary. Bring him to a room where he can sleep. We have ridden far."

"Aye, your honor!" the host bobbed and mumbled, rubbing his hands together; for Etienne had a way of impressing common folk with his importance, as if he were a count at the very least. But of that later.

The innkeeper shambled through a low ceilinged room adjoining the tap-room, and which opened out into another, more spacious room above. It was under the

steep roof, and barely furnished, but even so more
elaborate than anything to which I had ever been
accustomed. I saw—for somehow I had begun instinc-
tively to note such details—that the only entrance or
egress was through the door which opened on to the
ladder; there was but one window, and that too small even
to admit my lithe form. And there was no bolt for the door
from within. I saw Etienne scowl and shoot a quick
suspicious glance at the innkeeper, but that lout did not
seem to notice, rubbing his hands and discoursing on the
excellent qualities of the den into which he had brought
us.

"Sleep, brother," said Etienne for our host's benefit;
then as he turned away, he whispered in my ear, "I trust
him not; we will move on as soon as night falls. Rest
meantime. I will come for you at dusk."

Whether it was the wine, after all, or unsuspected
weariness, I cannot say; but laying myself down on the
straw pallet in my clothing, I fell asleep before I knew it,
and slumbered long.

2

WHAT WOKE me was the gentle opening of the door. I wakened to darkness, relieved but little by the starlight in the tiny window. No one spoke, but something moved in the darkness. I heard a beam creak and thought I caught the sounds of suppressed breathing.

"Is that you, Etienne?" I whispered. There was no answer, and I spoke a trifle louder. "Etienne! Is that you, Etienne Villiers?"

I thought I heard breath hiss softly between teeth, then the beam creaked again, and a stealthy shuffle receded from me. I heard the door open and close softly, and knew I was once more alone in the room. I sprang up, drawing my dagger. That had not been Etienne, coming for me as he had promised, and I wished to know who it was that had sought to creep upon me in the darkness.

Gliding to the door I opened it and gazed down into the

lower room. There was only darkness, as if I looked into a well, but I heard someone moving across the room, and then a fumbling at the outer door. Taking my dagger in my teeth, I slid silently down the ladder, with an ease and stealth that surprised myself. As my feet touched the floor and I seized my dagger and crouched in the darkness, I saw the outer door swing open, and a bulk was framed in the opening for an instant. I recognized the stooped top-heavy figure of the innkeeper. He was breathing so heavily that he could not have heard the faint sounds I made. He ran clumsily but quickly across the court-like space behind the tavern, and I saw him vanish into space behind the tavern, and I saw him vanish into the stables. I watched, straining my eyes in the dim starlight, and presently he came forth leading a horse. He did not mount the beast, but led him into the forest, showing every evidence of a desire for silence and secrecy. A short time after he had vanished, I caught the faint sound of a horse galloping. Evidently mine host had mounted after attaining a descreet distance from the inn, and was now riding hard to some unknown goal.

All I could think of was that somehow he recognized me, knew of me, and was riding to bear word to my father. I turned and opened the door a crack into the tap-room, and peered in. No one was there but the serving wench, asleep on the floor. A candle burned on the table, and moths fluttered about it. From somewhere there came a faint indistinct mumble of voices.

I glided out the back door and stole around the tavern. Silence hung over the black shadowed forest, except for a faint far cry of a night bird, and the restless movement of the great stallion in his stall.

Candle light streamed from the window of a small room on the other side of the tavern, separated from the common-room by a short passage. As I glided past this window, I halted suddenly, hearing my name spoken. I nestled close to the wall listening shamelessly. I heard the quick, clear though low-pitched voice of Etienne, and the rumble of another.

"—Agnes de Chastillon, she said. What does it matter what a peasant wench calls herself? Is she not a handsome baggage?"

"I've seen prettier in Paris, aye, and in Chartres, too," answered the rumbling voice; which came, I knew, from the fat man who had occupied the settle when we first entered the tavern.

"Pretty!" There was scorn in Etienne's voice. "The girl's more than pretty. There's something wild and untamable about her. Something fresh and vital, I tell you. Any worn-out noble would pay high for her; she would renew the youth of the most jaded debauchee. Look you, Thibault, I would not be offering you this prize, were it not that the risk is too great for me to ride on to Chartres with her. I am suspicious of this dog of an innkeeper, too."

"If he does recognize you as the man for whose head the Duc d'Alencon yearns—" muttered Thibault.

"Be quiet, fool!" hissed Etienne. "That is another reason I must be rid of the wench. I was surprised into telling her my true name. But by the saints, Thibault, my meeting with her was enough to jolt the calm of a saint! I rounded a bend in the road, and there she stood, straight and tall against the green wood in her torn wedding gown, with her blue eyes smoldering, and the rising sun glinting red in her hair and turning to a streak of blood the dagger in her hand! For an instant I doubted me if she were human, and a strange thrill, almost of terror, swept over me."

"A country wench in a woods road frightens Etienne Villiers, a rake among rakes," snorted Thibault, drinking from a jack with a loud sucking noise.

"She was more than that," retorted Etienne. "There was something fateful about her, like a figure in a tragic drama; something terrible. She is fair, yet there is something strange and dark about her. I cannot explain nor understand it."

"Enough, enough!" yawned Thibault. "You weave a romaunt about a Norman jade. Come to the point."

"I have come to it," snapped Etienne. "I had intended taking her on to Chartres and selling her to a brothel-keeper I wot of, myself; but I realize my folly. I would have to pass too close to the domain of the Duke of Alencon, and if he learned I was in the lands—"

"He has not forgotten," grunted Thibault. "He would pay high for information regarding your whereabouts. He dares not arrest you openly; it will be a dagger in the dark, a shot from the bushes. He would close your mouth in secrecy and silence, if he might."

"I know," snarled Etienne with a shudder. "I was a fool to come this far east. Dawn shall find me far away. But you can take the girl to Chartres without fear, aye, or to Paris, for that matter. Give me the price I ask, and she is yours."

"It is too high," protested Thibault. "Suppose she fights like a wildcat?"

"That is your look out," callously answered Etienne. "You have tamed enough wenches so you should be able to handle this one. Though I warn you, there is fire in the girl. But that is your business. You have told me your companions lie in a village not far from here. Get them to aid you. If you cannot make a pretty profit of her in Chartres, or in Orleans, or in Paris, you are a greater fool than I am."

"Well, well," grumbled Thibault. "I'll take a chance; after all, that is what a business man must do."

I heard the clink of silver coins on the table, and the sound was like a knell to me.

And indeed it was my knell for as I leaned blindly and sickly against the tavern wall, there died in me the girl I had been, and in her stead rose the woman I have become. My sickness passed, and cold fury turned me brittle as steel and pliant as fire.

"A drink to seal the bargain," I heard Etienne say; "then I must ride. When you go for the wench—"

I hurled open the door, and Etienne's hand froze with the goblet at his lips. Thibault's eyes bulged at me over the rim of his wine cup. A greeting died on Etienne's lips, and he went suddenly pale at the death in my eyes.

"Agnes!" he exclaimed, rising. I stepped through the door and my blade was sheathed in Thibault's heart before he could rise. An agonized grunt bubbled from his fat lips, and he sank from his bench, spurting red.

"Agnes!" cried Etienne again, throwing out his arms as if to fend me off. "Wait girl—"

"You filthy dog!" I screamed, blazing into mad fury. "You swine—swine—*swine!*" Only my own blind fury saved him as I rushed and stabbed.

I was on him before he could put himself into a position of defense, and my blindly driven steel tore the skin over his ribs. Thrice more I struck, silent and murderous, and he somehow fended the blade from his heart, though the point drew blood from hand, arm and shoulder. Desperately he grasped my wrist and sought to break it, and close-locked we tumbled against the table, over the edge of which he bent me and tried to strangle me. But to grasp my throat he must perforce my wrist with one hand, and twisting it free of his single grip, I struck for his life. The point snapped on a metal buckle and the jagged shard tore through doublet and shirt, and ploughed along his breast; blood spurted and a groan escaped him. In anguish his grasp weakened, and I twisted from beneath him and dealt him a buffet with my clenched fist that rocked back his head and brought streams of blood from his nostrils. Groping for me he clutched me, and as I gouged at his eyes, he hurled me from him with such force that I hurtled backward across the room and crashed into the wall, thence toppling to the floor.

I was half dazed, but I rebounded with a snarl, gripping a broken table leg. He was wiping blood from his eyes with one hand and fumbling for his sword with the other, but again he misjudged the speed of my attack, and the table leg crashed full on his crown, laying open the scalp and bringing blood in torrents. He threw up his arms to ward off the strokes, and on them and on his head I rained blow after blow, driving him backward, half bent, blind and reeling, until he crashed down into the ruins of the table.

"God, girl," he whimpered; "would you slay me?"

"With a joyful heart!" I laughed, as I had never laughed before, and I struck him over the ear, knocking him back down among the ruins out of which he was groping.

A moaning cry sobbed through his crushed lips. "In God's name, girl," he moaned, extending his hands blindly toward me, "have mercy! Hold your hand, in the name of the saints! I am not fit to die!"

He struggled to his knees, streaming blood from his battered head, his garments dripping crimson. "Hold your hand, Agnes," he croaked. "Pity, in God's name!"

I hesitated, staring somberly down at him. Then I threw aside my bludgeon.

"Take your life," I said in bitter scorn. "You are too poor a thing to stain my hands. Go your ways!"

He sought to rise, then sank down again.

"I cannot rise," he groaned. "The room swims to my gaze, and grows dark. Oh, Agnes, it is a bitter kiss you have given me! God have mercy on me, for I die in sin. I have laughed at death, but now that it is upon me, I am afraid. Ah, God, I fear! Leave me not, Agnes! Leave me not to die like a dog!"

"Why should I not?" I asked bitterly. "I trusted you, and thought you nobler than common men, with your lying words of chivalry and honor. Pah! You would have sold me into slavery viler than a Turk's harem."

"I know," he moaned. "My soul is blacker than the night that steals upon me. Call the innkeeper and let him fetch a priest."

"He is gone on some mission of his own," I answered. "He stole out the back door and rode into the forest."

"He is gone to betray me to the Duke of Alencon," muttered Etienne. "He recognized me, after all. I am indeed lost."

Now it came to me that it was because of my calling Etienne's name in the darkness of the room above that the innkeeper became aware of my false friend's true identity. So it might be said that if the Duke laid Etienne by the heels, it would be because of my unconscious betrayal. And like most country people, I had only fear and distrust of the nobility.

"I'll take you hence," I said. "Not even a dog shall fall into the hands of the law by my will."

I left the tavern hurriedly and went to the stables. Of the slattern I saw nothing. Either she had fled to the woods, or else was too drunk to heed. I saddled and bridled Etienne's stallion, though it laid back its ears and snapped and kicked at me, and led it to the door. Then I went within and spoke to Etienne; and indeed a fearsome sight he was, bruised and battered, with tattered doublet and shirt, and all covered with blood.

"I have brought your horse," I said.

"I cannot rise," he mumbled.

"Set your teeth," I commanded. "I will carry you."

"You can never do it, girl," he protested, but even as he spoke, I heaved him up on my shoulders and bore him through the door, and a dead weight he was, with limbs trailing like a dead man's. Getting him upon the horse was a heart-breaking task, for it was little he could do to aid himself, but at last it was accomplished, and I swung up behind the saddle and held him in place.

Then as I hesitated, in doubt as to where to go, he seemed to sense my uncertainty, for he mumbled: "Take the road westward, to Saint Girault. There is a tavern there, a mile this side the town, the Red Boar, whose keeper is my friend."

Of that ride through the night, I will speak but briefly. We met no one, riding through a ribbon of starlight, walled by black forest trees. My hand grew sticky with Etienne's blood, for the jolting of the pace set his many wounds to bleeding afresh, and presently he grew delirious and spake disjointedly of other times and people strange to me. Anon he mentioned names known to me by reputation, lords, ladies, soldiers, outlaws and pirates, and he raved of dark deeds and sordid crimes and feats of curious heroism. And betimes he sang snatches of marching songs and drinking songs and bawdy ballads and love lyrics, and maundered in alien tongues unintelligible to me. Ah—I have ridden many roads since that night, of intrigue or violence, but never stranger ride rode I than that ride in the night through the forest to Saint Girault.

Dawn was a hint in the branch-scarred sky when I drew up at a tavern I believed was the one Etienne meant. The picture on the board proved such to be the case, and I shouted for the keeper. A lout of a boy came forth in his shirt, yawning, and digging his fists into his sluggish eyes, and when he saw the great stallion and its riders, all dabbled and splashed with blood, he bawled with fear and amaze and scudded back into the tavern with his shirt tail flapping about his rump. Presently then a window was cautiously pushed open upstairs, and a night-capped head was thrust out behind the muzzle of a great arquebuse.

"Go your ways," quoth the night-cap; "we have no dealings with bandits and bloody murderers."

"Here are no bandits," I answered angrily, being weary and short of patience. "Here is a man who has been set upon and nearly slain. If you are the innkeeper of the Red Boar, he is a friend of yours—Etienne Villiers, of Aquitaine."

"Etienne!" exclaimed mine host. "I will be down. Assuredly I will be down. Why did you not say it was Etienne?"

The window slammed and there was a sound of stairs being rapidly descended. I slid from the stallion and received Etienne's toppling form in my arms, easing him to the ground as the keeper rushed forth with servants bearing torches.

Etienne lay like one dead, his face livid where it was not masked with blood, but his heart beat strongly, and I knew he was partly conscious.

"Who did this, in God's name?" demanded mine host in horror.

"I did," I answered shortly. He gave back from me, paling in the torchlight.

"God ha' mercy on us! A youth like—holy Denis protest us! It's a woman!"

"Enough of this babble!" I exclaimed, angered. "Take him up and bear him into your best chamber."

"B-b-but—" began mine host, still bewildered, while the menials backed away.

I stamped my foot and swore, which is a custom always common to me.

"Death of the devil and Judas Iscariot!" quoth I. "Will you allow your friend to die while you gape and stare? Take him up!" I laid hand on his dagger, which I had girdled to mine own waist, and they hastened to obey me, staring as though I were the arch-fiend's daughter.

"Etienne is always welcome," mumbled mine host, "but a she-devil in breeches—"

"You will wear your own longer if you talk less and work more," I assured him, plucking a bell-mouthed pistol from the girdle of a servant who was too frightened even to remember he had it. "Do as I say, and there will be no more slaying tonight. Onward!"

Eye, verily, the happenings of the night had matured me. I was not yet fully a woman, but on the way to being one.

They bore Etienne to what mine host—whose name was Perducas—swore was the best chamber in the tavern, and sooth to say, it was much finer than anything in the Knave's Fingers. It was an upper room, opening out upon the landing of a winding stair, and it had windows of a proper size, though no other door.

Perducas swore that he was as good a leech as any man, and we stripped Etienne and set to work reviving him. Indeed, he showed to be as roughly handled as any man I had ever seen, not to be mortally wounded. But when we had washed the blood and dust off his body, we found that none of his dagger-wounds had touched a vital spot, nor was his skull fractured, though the scalp had been split in several places. His right arm was broken and the other black with bruises, and the broken bone we set, I helping Perducas with some skill, for accidents and wounds had always been common enough in La Fere.

When we had his wounds bandaged, and him laid in a

clean bed, he recovered his senses enough to gulp wine and inquire where he was. When I told him, he muttered: "Leave me not, Agnes; Perducas is a man among men, but I require a woman's tender care."

"Saint Denis deliver me from such tender care as this hell-cat has shown," quoth Perducas under his breath. And I said: "I will remain until you are upon your feet again, Etienne." And he seemed satisfied therewith, and went into a calm slumber.

I then demanded a room for myself, and Perducas, having sent a boy to attend the stallion, showed me a chamber adjoining that of Etienne's, though not connected with it by any door. I laid myself down on the bed just as the sun was coming up, it being the first feather bed I had ever seen, much less lain on, and slept for many hours.

When I came again to Etienne, I found him in full possession of his senses, and free of delirium. Indeed, in those days men were iron, and if their wounds were not instantly mortal, they quickly recovered, unless their hurts became poisoned through the carelessness or ignorance of the leeches. Perducas would have none of the nauseous and childish remedies praised by the physicians, but divers clean herbs and plants he gathered in the depths of the woods. He told me that he learned his art from the *hakims* of the Saracens, among whom he had traveled in his youth. He was a man of many unexpected sides, was Perducas.

Together he and I tended Etienne, who healed rapidly. Little speech passed between us. He and Perducas talked much together, but most of the time Etienne merely lay and looked silently at me.

Perducas talked to me a little, but seemed to fear me. When I spoke of my score, he replied that I owed him naught; that as long as Etienne desired my presence, food and lodging were mine, without pay. But he earnestly desired me not to converse with the towns' people, lest their curiosity lead to the discovery of Etienne. His servants, he said, could be trusted to silence. I asked him naught of the reason for the Duc d'Alencon's hatred for Etienne, but quoth he: "It is no common score which the Duke holdeth against Etienne Villiers. Etienne was once in this nobleman's train, and was unwise enough to perform for him a most delicate mission. D'Alencon is ambitious; 'tis whispered that naught but the rank of constable of France will satisfy him. He is now high in favor with the king; that favor might not shine with such lustre were it known what letters once passed between the Duke and Charles of Germany, whom men now know as the emperor of the Holy Roman Empire.

"Etienne alone knows the full extent of that plotted treason. Therefore d'Alencon burns for Etienne's death, yet dares not strike openly, lest his victim damn him forever with his dying breath. He would strike subtly and silently, by hidden dagger, poison or ambush. As long as Etienne is within his reach, Etienne's only safety lies in secrecy."

"Suppose there are others like that rogue Thibault?" I demanded.

"Nay," quoth he. "'Tis no doubt there are. I know that band of gallows' bait well. But 'tis their one point of honor that they betray not one of comrades. And in time past Etienne was one of them—cut-purses, women-snatchers, thieves and murderers that they are."

I shook my head, musing on the strangeness of men, insomuch that Perducas, an honest man, was friend to a rogue like Etienne, knowing well his villainies. Well, many an honest man secretely admires a rogue, seeing in him that which he himself would be, if he lacked not the courage.

Ah well, I heeded well Perducas' desires, and time dragged heavily on my hands. I seldom left the tavern, save at night, and then only to wander in the woods, avoiding the people of the countryside and of the market-town. And a growing restlessness stirred me, and a feeling that I was waiting for something I knew not what, and that I be up and doing—I knew not what. A week had passed in this manner, when I met Guiscard de Clisson.

3

Beyond the creak of rat-gnawed beams in squalid peasant huts:
  Above the groan of ox-wain wheels that ground the muddy rats:
I heard the beat of distant drums that call me night and day.
  To roads where armored captains ride, in steel and roses panoplied,
With banners flowing crimson-dyed—over the world away!

—Drums in My Ears

I entered into the tavern one morning, after an early walk in the woods, and halted at the sight of the stranger gnawing a beef-bone at the board. He too stopped short in his gorging and stared at me. He was a tall man, rangy and hard of frame. A scar seamed his lean features, and his grey eyes were cold as steel. He was, indeed, a man of steel, clad in cuirass, thigh-pieces and greaves. His broadsword lay across his knees, his morion rested on the bench beside him.

"By God!" quoth he. "Are you man or woman?"

"What do you think?" I asked, leaning my hands on the board and looking down at him.

"Only a fool would ask the question I asked," said he, with a shake of his head. "You are all woman; yet your attire strangely becomes you. A pistol in your girdle, too. You remind me of a woman I once knew; she marched and fought like a man, and died of a pistol ball on the field of battle. She was dark where you are fair, but there is something similar in the set of your chin, in your carriage—nay, I know not. Sit ye down and converse with me. I am Guiscard de Clisson. Have you heard of me?"

"Many a time," I answered, seating myself. "In my native village they tell tales of you. You are a leader of mercenaries and Free Companions."

"When men have guts enough to be led," quoth he, quaffing, and holding out the flagon to me. "Ha, by the tripe and blood of Judas, you guzzle like a man! Mayhap women are becoming men, for 'tis truth, by Saint Trignan, that men are become women, these days. Not a recruit for my company have I gained in this province, where, in days I can remember, men fought for the honor of following a captain of mercenaries. Death of Satan! With the Emperor gathering his accursed Lanzknecht to sweep de Lautrec out of Milan, and the king in such dire need of soldiers—to say nothing of the rich loot in Italy—every able-bodied Frenchman ought to be marching southward, by God! Ah, for the old-time spirit of men!"

Now as I looked at this war-scarred veteran, and heard his talk, my heart beat quick with a strange longing, and I seemed to hear, as I had heard so often in my dreams, the distant beating of drums.

"I will ride with you!" I exclaimed. "I am weary of being a woman. I will make one of your company!"

He laughed and slapped the board with his open hand, as if at a great jest.

"By Saint Denis, girl," quoth he, "you have a proper spirit, but it take more than a pair of breeches to make a man."

"If that other woman of whom you spoke could march and fight, so can I!" I cried.

"Nay." He shook his head. "Black Margot of Avignon was one in a million. Forget this foolish fancy, girl. Don thy petticoats and become a proper woman once more. Then—well, in your proper place I might be glad to have you ride with me!"

Ripping out an oath that made him start, I sprang up, knocking my bench backward so it fell with a crash. I stood before him, clenching and unclenching my hands, seething with the rage that always rose quickly in me.

"Ever the man in men!" I said between my teeth. "Let a woman know her proper place: let her milk and spin and sew and bake and bear children, not look beyond her threshold or the command of her lord and master! Bah! I spit on you all! There is no man alive who can face me with weapons and live, and before I die, I'll prove it to the world. Women! Cows! Slaves! Whimpering, cringing serfs, crouching to blows, revenging themselves by— taking their own lives, as my sister urged me to do. Ha! You deny me a place among men? By God, I'll live as I please and die as God wills, but if I'm not fit to be a man's comrade, at least I'll be no man's mistress. So go ye to hell, Guiscard de Clisson, and may the devil tear your heart!"

So saying I wheeled and strode away, leaving him gaping after me. I mounted the stair and came into Etienne's chamber, where I found him lying on his bed, much improved, though still pale and weak, and his arm like to be in its sling for weeks to come.

"How fares it with you?" I demanded.

"Well enough," he answered, and after staring at me a space: "Agnes," said he, "why did you spare my life when you could have taken it?"

"Because of the woman in me," I answered morosely; "that cannot bear to hear a helpless thing beg for life."

"I deserved death at your hands," he muttered "more than Thibault. Why have you tended and cared for me?"

"I did not wish you to fall into the hands of the Duke because of me," I answered, "since it was I who unwittingly betrayed you. And now you have asked me these questions, I will e'en ask you one; why be such a damnable rogue?"

"God knows," he answered, closing his eyes. "I have never been anything else, as far back as I can remember, and my memory runs back to the gutters of Poitiers, where I snatched for crusts and lied for pennies as a child, and got my first knowledge of the ways of the world. I have been soldier, smuggler, pander, cut-throat, thief— always a black rogue. Saint Denis, some of my deeds have been too black to repeat. And yet somewhere, somehow, there has always been an Etienne Villiers hidden deep in the depths of the creature that is myself, untarnished by the rest of me. There lies remorse and fear, and makes for misery. So I begged for life when I should have welcomed death, and now lie here speaking truth when I should be framing lies for your seduction. Would I were all saint or all rogue."

At that instant feet stamped on the stair, and rough voices rose. I sprang to bar the door, hearing Etienne's name called, but he halted me with a lifted hand, harkened, then sank back with a sigh of relief.

"Nay, I recognize the voice. Enter, comrades!" he called.

Then into the chamber trooped a foul and ruffianly band, led by a pot-bellied rogue in enormous boots. Behind him came four others, ragged, scarred, with cropped ears, patched eyes, or flattened noses. They leered at me, and then glared at the man on the bed.

"So, Etienne Villiers," said the fat rogue, "we ha' fund ye! Hiding from us is not so easy as hiding from the Duc d'Alencon, eh, you dog?"

"What manner of talk is this, Tristan Pelligny?" demanded Etienne, in unfeigned astonishment. "Have you come to greet a wounded comrade, or—"

"We have come to do justice on a rat!" roared Pelligny. He turned and ponderously indicated his ragamuffin crew, pointing a thick forefinger at each. "See ye here, Etienne Villiers? Jacques of the Warts, Gaston the Wolf, Jehan Crop-ear, and Conrad the German. And myself maketh five, good men and true, once your comrades, come to do justice upon you for foul murder!"

"You are mad!" exclaimed Etienne, struggling upon his elbows. "Whom have I murdered that you should be wroth thereat? When I was one of you did I not always bear my share of the toil and dangers of thievery, and divide the loot fairly?"

"We talk not now of loot!" bellowed Tristan. "We speak of our comrade Thibault Bazas, foully murdered by you in the tavern of the Knave's Fingers!"

Etienne's mouth started open, he hesitated, glanced in a startled way at me, then closed his mouth again. I started forward.

"Fools!" I exclaimed. "He did not slay that fat swine Thibault. *I* killed him."

"Saint Denis!" laughed Tristan. " 'Tis the wench in the breeches of whom the slattern spoke! You slew Thibault? Ha! A pretty lie, but not convincing, to any whom knew Thibault. The serving wench heard the fighting, and fled in fright into the forest. When she dared to return, Thibault lay dead, and Etienne and his jade were riding away together. Nay, 'tis too plain. Etienne slew Thibault, doubtless over this very hussy. Well, when we have disposed of him, we will take care of his leman, eh lads?"

A babble of profane and obscene agreement answered him.

"Agnes," said Etienne, "call Perducas."

"Call and be damned," said Tristan. "Perducas and all the servants are out in the stable, drenching Guiscard de Clisson's nag. We'll have our task done before they return. Here—stretch his traitor out on yonder bench. Before I cut his throat, I'd fain try my knife edge on other parts of him."

He brushed me aside contemptuously, and strode to Etienne's bed, followed close by the others. Etienne struggled upright, and Tristan struck him with clenched fist, knocking him down again. In that instant the room swam red in my gaze. With a leap I had Etienne's sword in my hand and at the feel of the hilt, power and a strange confidence rushed like fire through my veins.

With a fierce exultant cry I ran at Tristan, and he wheeled, bellowing, fumbling at his sword. I cut that bellow short as my sword sheared through his thick neck muscles and he went down, spouting blood, his head hanging by a shred of flesh. The other ruffians gave tongue like a pack of hounds and turned on me in fear and fury. And remembering suddenly the pistol in my girdle, I plucked it forth and fired point-blank into the face of Jacques, blasting his skull into a red ruin. In the hanging smoke the others made at me, bawling foul curses.

There are actions to which we are born, and for which we have a talent exceeding mere teaching. I, who had never before had a sword in my grasp, found it like a living thing in my hand, wielded by unguessed instinct. And I found, again, my quickness of eye and hand and foot was not to be matched by these dull clods. They bellowed and flailed blindly, wasting strength and motion, as if their swords were cleavers, while I smote in deadly silence, and with deadly certainty.

I do not remember much of that fight; it is a crimson haze in which a few details stand out. My thoughts were moving too swiftly for my brain to record, and I know not fully how, with what leaps, ducks, side-steps and parries I avoided those flailing blades. I know that I split the head of Conrad the German, as a man splits a melon, and his brains gushed sickeningly over the blade. And I remember that the one called Gaston the Wolf trusted too much in a brigandine he wore among his rags, and that under my desperate stroke, the rusty links burst and he fell upon the floor with his bowels spilling out. Then as in red cloud, only Jehan was rushing at me, and flailing down with his sword. And I caught his descending wrist on my edge. His hand, holding the sword, jumped from his wrist on an arch of crimson, and as he stared stupidly at the spouting stump, I ran him through with such ferocity that the cross-piece struck hard against his breast, and I pitched over him as he fell.

I do not remember rising and wrenching free my blade. On wide braced legs, sword trailing, I reeled among the corpses, then a deadly sickness overcame me, and I staggered to the window and leaning my head over the sill, retched fearfully. I found that blood was streaming down my arm from a slash in my shoulder, and my shirt was in ribbons. The room swam to my gaze, and the scent of fresh blood, swimming in the entrails of the slain, revolted me. As if through a mist I saw Etienne's white face.

Then there came a pound of feet on the stair and Guiscard de Clisson burst through the door, sword in hand, followed by Perducas. They stared like men struck dead, and de Clisson swore appallingly.

"Did I not tell you?" gasped Perducas. "The devil in breeches! Saint Denis, what a slaughter!"

"Is this your work, girl?" asked Guiscard in a strange small voice. I shook back my damp hair and struggled to my feet, swaying dizzily.

"Aye; it was a debt I had to pay."

"By God!" muttered he, staring. "There is something dark and strange about you, for all your fairness."

"Aye, Dark Agnes!" said Etienne, lifting himself on elbow. "A star of darkness shone on her birth, of darkness and unrest. Where ever she goes shall be blood spilling and men dying. I knew it when I saw her standing against the sunrise that turned to blood the dagger in her hand."

"I have paid my debt to you," I said. "If I placed your life in jeopardy, I have bought it back with blood." And casting his dripping sword at his feet, I turned toward the door.

Guiscard, who had been staring like one daft, shook himself as if from a trance, and strode after me.

"Nails of the Devil!" quoth he. "What has just passed has altered my mind entirely! You are such another as Black Margot of Avignon. A true sword-woman is worth a score of men. Would you still march with me?"

"As a companion-in-arms," I answered. "I'm mistress to none."

"None save Death," he answered, glancing at the corpses.

4

Her sisters bend above their looms
And gnaw their moldy crumbs:
But she rides forth in silk and steel
To follow the phantom drums.
—The Ballad of Dark Agnes.

A WEEK after the fight in Etienne's chamber, Guiscard de Clisson and I rode from the tavern of the Red Boar and took the road to the east. I bestrode a mettlesome destrier and was clad as became a comrade of de Clisson. Velvet doublet and silk trunk-hose I wore, with long Spanish boots; beneath my doubtlet plaint steel mail guarded red locks. Pistols were in my girdle, and a sword hung from a richly-worked baldrie. Over all was flung a cloak of crimson silk. These things Guiscard had purchased for me, swearing when I protested at his lavishness.

"Cans't pay me back from the loot we take in Italy," said he. "But a comrade of Guiscard de Clisson go bravely clad!"

Sometimes I misdoubt me that Guiscard's acceptance of me as a man was as complete as he would have had me think. Perchance he still secretly cherished his original idea—no matter.

47

That week had been a crowded one. For hours each day Guiscard had instructed me in the art of swordsmanship. He himself was accounted the finest blade in France, and he swore that he had never encountered apter pupil than I. I learned the rogueries of the blade as if I had been born to it, and the speed of my eye and hand often brought amazed oaths from his lips. For the rest, he had me shoot at marks with pistol and matchlock, and showed me many crafty and savage tricks of hand to hand fighting. No novice had ever more able teacher; no teacher had ever more eager pupil. I was afire with the urge to learn all pertaining to the trade. I seemed to have been born into a new world, and yet a world for which I was intended from birth. My former life seemed like a dream, soon to be forgotten.

So that early morning, the sun not yet up, we swung on to our horses in the courtyard of the Red Boar, while Perducas bade us God-speed. As we reined around, a voice called my name, and I perceived a white face at an upper casement.

"Agnes!" cried Etienne. "Are you leaving without so much as bidding me farewell?"

"Why should there be such ceremony between us?" I asked. "There is no debt on either side. There should be no friendship, as far as I can see. You are well enough to tend yourself, and need my care no longer."

And saying no more, I reined away and rode with Guiscard up the winding forest road. He looked at me sidewise and shrugged his shoulders.

"A strange woman you are, Dark Agnes," quoth he. "You seem to move through life like one of the Fates, unmoved, unchangeable, potent with tragedy and doom. I think men who ride with you will not live long."

I did not reply, and so we rode on through the green wood. The sun came up, flooding the leaves with gold as they swayed in the morning wind; a deer flashed across the path ahead of us, and the birds were chanting their joy of Life.

We were following the road over which I had carried Etienne after the fight in the Knave's Fingers, but toward midday we turned off on another, broader road which slanted southeastward. Nor had we ridden far, after the turn, when: "Where man is not 'tis peaceful enough," quoth Guiscard, then: "What now?"

A fellow snoozing beneath a tree had woken, started up, stared at us, and then turning quickly aside, plunged among the great oaks which lined the road, and vanished. I had but a glimpse of him, seeing that he was an ill-visaged rogue, wearing the hood and smock of a wood-cutter.

"Our martial appearance frightened the clown," laughed Guiscard, but a strange uneasiness possessed me, causing me to stare nervously at the green forest walls that hemmed us in.

"There are no bandits in this forest," I muttered. "He had no cause to flee from us. I like it not. Hark!"

A high, shrill, quavering whistle rose in the air, from somewhere out among the trees. After a few seconds it was answered by another, far to the east, faint with distance. Straining my ears, I seemed to catch yet a third response, still further on.

"I like it not," I repeated.

"A bird calling its mate," he scoffed.

"I was born and raised in the forest," I answered impatiently. "Yonder was no bird. Men are signalling one another out there in the forest. Somehow I believe 'tis connected with that rogue who fled from the path."

"You have the instincts of an old soldier," laughed Guiscard, doffing his helmet for the coolness and hanging it on his saddle bow. "Suspicious—alert— 'tis well enough. But your wariness is wasted in this wood, Agnes. I have no enemies hereabouts. Nay, I am well known and friend to all. And since there are no robbers nigh, it follows that we have naught to fear from anyone."

"I tell you," I protested as we rode on, "I have a haunting presentiment that all is not well. Why should that rogue run from us, and then whistle to some hidden mate as we passed? Let us leave the road and take to a path."

By this time we had passed some distance beyond where we had heard the first whistle, and had entered a broken region traversed by a shallow river. Here the road broadened out somewhat, though still walled by thick trees and bushes. On the left hand the bushes grew densely, close to the road. On the right hand they were straggling, bordering a shallow stream whose opposite bank rose in sheer cliffs. The brush-grown space between road and stream was perhaps a hundred paces broad.

"Agnes, girl," Guiscard was saying, "I tell thee, we are as safe as—"

Crash! A thundering volley ripped out of the bushes on the left, masking the road with whirling smoke. My horse screamed and I felt him stagger. I saw Guiscard de Clisson throw up his hands and sway backward in his saddle, then his horse reared and fell with him. All this I saw in a brief instant, for my horse bolted, crashing frantically through the bushes on the right hand side of the road, and a branch knocked me from the saddle, to lie half stunned among the bushes.

As I lay there, unable to see the road for the denseness of the covert, I heard loud rough voices, and the sound of men coming out of their ambush into the road.

"Dead as Judas Iscariot!" bawled one. "Where did the wench go?"

"Yonder goes her horse, splashing across the stream,

gushing blood, and with empty saddle," quoth another. "She fell among the bushes somewhere."

"Would we could have taken her alive," said yet another. "She would have furnished rare sport. But take no chances, the Duke said. Ah, here is Captain d'Valence!"

There was a drumming of hoofs up the road, and the rider shouted: "I heard the volley, where is the girl?"

"Lying dead among the bushes somewhere," he was answered. "Here is the man."

An instance silence, then: "Thunders of hell!" roared the captain. "Fools! Bunglers! Dogs! *This is not Etienne Villiers!* You've murdered Guiscard de Clisson!"

A babble of confusion rose, curses, accusations and denials, dominated by the voice of him they called d'Valence.

"I tell you, I would know de Clisson in hell, and this is he, for all his head is a mass of blood. Oh, you fools!"

"We but obeyed orders," another growled. "When you heard the signal, you put us in ambush and bade us shoot who ever came down the road. How did we know who it was we were to murder? You never spoke his name; our business was but to shoot the man you should designate. Why did you not remain with us and see it well done?"

"Because this is the Duke's service, fool!" snapped d'Valence. "I am too well known. I could not take the chance of being seen and recognized, if the ambush failed."

They then turned on some one else. There was the sound of a blow, and yelp of pain.

"Dog!" swore d'Valence. "Did you not give the signal that Etienne Villiers was riding this way?"

"'Tis not my fault!" howled the wretch, a peasant by his accent. "I knew him not. The taverner of the Knave's Fingers bade me watch for a man riding with a red-haired wench in a man's garb, and when I saw her riding by with the soldier, I thought he must be this Etienne Villiers—ahhh—mercy!"

There was a report, a shriek and the sound of a falling body.

"We will hang for this, if the Duke learns of it," said the captain. "Guiscard was high in the favor of the Vicomte de Lautrec, governor of Milan. D'Alencon will hang us to conciliate the Vicomte. We must guard our own necks. We will hide the bodies in the stream, and none will be the wiser. Scatter now, and look for the corpse of the girl. If she still lives, we must close her mouth for ever."

At that, I began to edge my way backwards, towards the stream. Glancing across, I saw that the opposite bank was low and level, grown with bushes, and walled by the cliffs I have mentioned, in which I saw what looked like the mouth of a ravine. That seemed to offer a way of retreat. Crawling until I came nearly to the water's edge, I rose and ran lightly toward the stream, which glided over a rocky bed scarcely knee-deep there. The bravos had spread out in a sort of crescent, beating the bushes. I heard them behind me, and, further away, on either side of me. And suddenly one gave tongue like a hound who sights the prey.

"There she goes! Halt, damn you!"

A matchlock cracked and the bullet whined past my ear, but I ran fleetly on. They came crashing and roaring through the bushes after me—a dozen men in morions and cuirasses, with swords in their hands.

One broke cover on the very edge of the stream, as I was splashing across, and fearing a thrust in the back, I turned and met him in midstream. He came on splashing like a bull, a great, whiskered, roaring swashbuckler, sword in hand.

We fell to it, thrusting, slashing and parrying, in water

knee-deep, and I was at disadvantage, for the swirling stream hindered my foot-work. His sword beat down on my helmet, making sparks glint before my eyes, and seeing the others closing in, I cast all on a desperate attack, and drove my sword so fiercely through his teeth that the point transfixed his skull and rang on the lining of his morion.

I wrenched my blade free as he sank down, crimsoning the stream, and even at that instant a pistol ball struck me in the thigh. I staggered, then recovered myself and limped swiftly out of the water and across the shore. The bravos were across the stream, bawling threats and waving their swords. Some loosed pistols at me, but their aim was vile, and I reached the cliff, dragging my injured leg. My boot was full of blood, and the whole limb numbed.

I plunged through the bushes at the mouth of the ravine—then halted with icy despair gripping my heart. I was in a trap. It was no ravine into which I had come, but merely a wide cleft in the rock of the cliff, which ran back a few yards and then narrowed to a crack. It formed a sharp triangle, the walls of which were too high and sheer to be climbed, wounded leg or no.

The bravos realized my plight, and came on with shouts of triumph. Dropping on my uninjured knee, behind the bushes at the cleft's mouth, I drew pistol and shot the foremost ruffian through the head. That halted their rush and sent them scattering for cover. Those on the other side of the stream ducked back into the trees, while those who had gained this side spread out among the bushes near the bank.

I reloaded my pistol and lay close, while they bawled to one another, and began loosing at my covert with matchlocks. But the heavy balls whined high over head or spattered futilely on the rocky walls, and presently, noting a black-whiskered rogue squirming across an open space toward a bush nearer my retreat, I put a ball through his body, whereat the others yelled blood-thirstily and renewed their fire. But the range was too far for those across the stream to do good shooting, and the others were shooting from difficult angles, not daring to show any part of themselves.

Presently one shouted: "Why do not some of you bastards go down stream and find a place to climb the cliff, and so come at the wench from above?"

"Because we could not injure her without showing ourselves," answered d'Valence from his covert; "and she shoots like the devil himself. Wait! Night will soon fall, and in the darkness she can not aim. She cannot escape. When it is too dusky for good shooting, we'll rush her and finish this matter with the steel. The bitch is wounded, I know. Bide your time!"

I chanced a long shot at the bushes whence d'Valence's voice issued, and from the burst of scorching profanity evoked thereby, do guess that my lead came too close for comfort.

Then followed a period of waiting, punctuated now and then by a shot from the trees. My injured leg throbbed, and flies gathered in a cloud about me. The sun, which had at first beat down fiercely into the crevice, withdrew, leaving me in deep shade, for which I was thankful. But hunger bit me, until my thirst grew so fierce that it drove hunger from mind. The sight and rippling noise of the stream nigh maddened. And the ball in my thigh burned so intolerably that I made shift to cut it out with my dagger, and then stanched the bleeding by cramming crumpled leaves into the wound.

I saw no way out; it seemed I must die there, perish all my dreams of pageantry and glory and the bright splendor and adventure. The dim drums whose beat I had sought to follow seemed fading and receding, like a distant knell, leaving only the dying ashes of death and oblivion.

But when I searched my soul for fear I found it not, nor regret nor any sorrow. Better to die there than live and grow old as the women I had known had grown old. I thought of Guiscard de Clisson, lying beside his dead horse, with his head in a pool of blood, and knew regret that death had come to him in such a sorry way, and that he had not died as he would have wished, on a field of battle, with the banner of his king flowing above him, and the blast of the trumpets in his ears.

The slow hours dragged on. Once I thought I heard a horse galloping, but the sound faded and ceased. I shifted my numb body and cursed the gnats, wishing mine enemies would charge while there was yet enough light for shooting.

Then, even as I heard them begin to shout to each other in the gathering dusk, a voice above and behind me brought me about, pistols raised, thinking they had climbed the cliff after all.

"Agnes!" The voice was low and urgent. "Hold your fire! It is I, Etienne!" The bushes were thrust aside, and a pale face looked over the brink of the cleft.

"Back, fool!" I exclaimed. "They'll shoot you like a pigeon!"

"They cannot see me from where they hide," he assured. "Speak softly, girl. Look, I lower this rope. It is knotted. Can you climb? I can never haul you up, with but one good arm."

Quick hope fired my nerves.

"Aye!" I hissed. "Let it down swiftly, and make the end fast. I hear them splashing across the stream."

Quickly then, in the gathering darkness, a snaky length came sliding down the cliff, and I laid hands upon it.

Crooking a knee about it, I dragged myself up hand over hand, and sinew-stretching work it was, for the lower end of the rope dangled free, and I turned like a pendulum. Then the whole task must be done by my hands alone, for my injured leg was stiff as a sword sheath, and anyway, my Spanish boots were not made for rope-climbing.

But I accomplished it, and dragged myself over the lip of cliff just as the cautious scrape of leather on sand, and the clink of steel told me that the bravos were gathering close to the crevice mouth for the rush.

Etienne swiftly gathered up the rope, and motioning to me, led the way through the bushes, talking in a hurried, nervous undertone. "I heard the shooting as I came along the road; left my horse tied in the forest and stole forward on foot to see what was forward. I saw Guiscard lying dead in the road, and understood from the shouts of the bravos that you were at bay. I know this place from of old. I stole back to my horse, rode along the stream until I found a place where I could ride up on the cliffs through a ravine. The rope I made of my cloak, torn to strips and spliced with my girdle and bridle-reins. Hark!"

Behind and below us broke out a mad clamor of yells and oaths.

"D'Alencon yearns indeed for my head," muttered Etienne. "I heard the bravos' talk while I crouched among the trees. Every road within leagues of Alencon is being patrolled by such bands as these since that dog of an inn keeper divulged to the Duke that I was again in this part of the kingdom.

"And now you will be hunted as desperately. I know Renault d'Valence, captain of those rogues. So long as he lives, your life will not be safe, for he will endeavor to destroy all proof that it was his knaves who slew Guiscard de Clisson. Here is my horse. We must not tarry."

"But why did you follow me?" I asked.

He turned and faced me, a pale-faced shadow in the dusk.

"You were wrong when you said no debt lay between us," quoth he. "I owe you my life. It was for me that you fought and slew Tristan Pelligny and his thieves. Why cling to your old hatred of me? You have well avenged a plotted wrong. You accepted Guiscard de Clisson as comrade. Will you not let me ride to the wars with you?"

"As comrade, no more," I said. "Remember, I am woman no longer."

"As brothers-in-arms," he agreed.

I thrust forth my hand, and he his, and our fingers locked briefly.

"Once more we must ride both on the same horse," he laughed, with a gay lilt of his old-time spirit. "Let us begone before those dogs find their way up here. D'Alencon has blocked the roads to Chartres, to Paris and to Orleans, but the world is ours! I think there are brave times ahead of us, adventures and wars and plunder! Then hey for Italy, and all brave adventurers!"

BLADES FOR FRANCE

Who I Met Men Wearing Masks

"STRIPLING, what do you with a sword? Ha, by Saint Denis, it's a woman! A woman with sword and helmet!"

And the great black-whiskered rogue halted with hand on hilt and gaped at me in amaze.

I gave back his stare no whit abashed. A woman, yes, and it was a lonely place, a shadow forest glade far from human habitation. But I did not wear doublet, trunk-hose and Spanish boots merely to show off my figure, and the morion perched on my red locks and the sword that hung at my hip were not ornaments.

I looked at this fellow whom chance had caused me to meet in the forest, and I liked him little. He was big enough, with an evil, scarred face; his morion was chased with gold, and under his cloak glimmered breastplate and gussets. This cloak was a notable garment, of Ciprus velvet, cunningly worked with gold thread. Apparently the owner had been napping under a huge tree nearby. A great horse stood there, tied to a branch, with rich housings of red leather and gilt braid. At the sight I sighed, for I had walked far since dawn, and my feet in my long boots ached.

"A woman!" repeated this rogue wonderingly. "And clad like a man! Throw off that tattered cloak, wench; I'd have a better sight of thee! Zounds, but you are a fine, tall, supple hussy! Come, doff your cloak!"

"Dog, have done!" I admonished harshly. "I'm no whimpering doxy for your sport."

"Who, then?" he ogled.

"Agnes de La Fere," I answered. "If you were not a stranger here, you'd know of me."

He shook his head. "Nay, I'm new come in these parts. I hail from Chalons, I. But no matter. One name's as good as another. Come hither, Agnes, and give me a kiss."

"Fool!" My ever ready anger was beginning to smolder. "Must I slay half the men in France to teach them respect? Look ye! I wear these garments but as the garbs and tools of my trade, not to catch the attention of men. I drink, fight and live like a man—"

"But shalt love like a woman!" quoth he, and lunging suddenly at me like a great bear, he sought to drag me into his embrace, but reeled back from a buffet that split his lip and brought a stream of blood down his black beard.

"Bitch!" he roared in swift fury, his eyes blazing. "I'll cripple you for that!" He made at me again with his great hands clutching, but as I wrenched out my sword, suddenly he seemed sobered by what he saw in my eyes, and, as if he realized at last that this was no play, he gave back and drew his own blade, casting off his cloak.

Our blades met with a clash that woke the echoes through the forest, and I came near killing him at the first pass. It was mainly by chance that he partially parried my fierce thrust, and as it was my point ploughed along his jaw-bone, so the blood gushed over his gorget. He yelled like a mad dog, but the wound steadied him, and made him realize that it was no child's task he had before him.

He wielded his blade with all his strength and craft, and no mean swordsman I found him. Well for me that I had learned the art from the finest blade in France, for this black-bearded rogue was mighty and cunning, and full of foul tricks and murderous subterfuges, whereby I knew he was no honest man, but a bravo, one of those hired killers who sell their swords to any who can pay their wage.

But I was no child at the game, and my quickness of eye and hand and foot was such as no man could match. Failing in all his tricks and strategy, Blackbeard sought to beat me down by sheer strength, raining thunderous blows on my guard with all his power. But this availed him no better, because, woman though I was, I was all steel springs and whale-bone, and had the art of turning his strokes before they were well begun, and thus avoiding their full fury. Presently his breath began to whistle through his bared teeth, and foam to mingle with the blood on his whiskers, and his belly to heave beneath his cuirass.

Then as his strength and fury began to fail, I attacked relentlessly, and beating down his weakening guard, drove my point into the midst of his black beard, above his gorget, severing jugular, wind pipe and spine at one thrust, so he gasped out his life even as he fell.

Cleansing my blade, I meditated upon my next action, and presently emptied out his pouch, finding a few silver coins therein, and I was disappointed at the poorness thereof, for I was without money, and hungry. Still, they would suffice for a supper at some woodland inn. Then, seeing that my cloak was, as he had said, worn and ragged, I took his, which I much admired because of the

curious quality of the gold thread which decorated it.
When I lifted it a mask of black silk fell out of it, and I
thought to leave it where it fell, but thought better of it,
and thrust it under my girdle. I wrapped the body in my
old cloak and dragged it into the bushes, where it would
not be seen by any chance passer-by, and mounting the
horse, rode on in the direction I had been travelling, and
very grateful for the easing of my weary feet.

As I pushed on through the gathering dusk, I fell to
brooding on the events which had befallen me since I, as
an ignorant country girl, had knifed the man my father
was forcing me to marry, and had fled the village of La
Fere, to become a swordwoman, and a swashbuckler in
breeches.

Truly, violence and death seemed to dog my trail.
Guiscard de Clisson, who taught me the art of the sword,
and with whom I was riding to the wars in Italy, had been
shot down from ambush by bravos hired by the Duc
d'Alencon, thinking him to be my friend Etienne Villiers.
Etienne had knowledge of intrigue against King Francis
on the part of the Duke, and for that knowledge his life
was forfeit. Now I too was being hunted by Renault
d'Valence, the leader of those bravos, since they thought
me to be the only one besides themselves who knew the
true facts of de Clisson's murder.

For d'Valence knew that if it were known that he and
his bravos had slain de Clisson, the famous general of the
mercenaries, d'Alencon would hang them all to pacify de
Clisson's friends. Guiscard's body was rotting in the river
where the bravos had thrown it, and now d'Valence was
hunting me on his own account, even while he hunted
Etienne for the Duke.

Villiers and I had run and hidden and dodged like rats
from the dogs, desirous of getting into Italy, but so far
being penned in that corner of the world through fear of

our enemies, who combed the kingdom for us. Even now I was on my way to a rendezvous with Etienne, who had gone stealthily to the coast, there to find, if he could, a certain pirate named Roger Hawksly, an Englishman, who harried the shores, for to such extremities were we forced that it was imperative that we get out of the country, however we could, since it was certain that we could not forever avoid the bloodhounds on our trail. I was to meet my companion at midnight, at a certain spot on the road that meandered down to the coast.

But as I rode through the twilight, I found no regret in my heart that I had traded my life of drudgery for one of wandering and violence. It was the life for which mysterious Fate had intended me, and I fitted it as well as any man: drinking, brawling, gambling, and fighting. With pistol, dagger or sword I had proved my prowess again and again, and I feared no man who walked the earth. Better a short life of adventure and wild living than a long dreary grind of soul-crushing household toil and child-bearing, cringing under the cudgel of a man I hated.

So I meditated as I came upon a small tavern set beside the forest road, the light of which set my empty belly to quivering anew. I approached warily, but saw none within the common room except the tap-boy and a serving wench, so gave my horse into the care of a stable-boy, and strode into the tavern.

The tap-boy gaped as he brought me a tankard of wine, and the wench stared until her eyes were like to pop out of her head, but I was used to such looks, and I merely bade her bring me food, and sat me down at the board, with my cloak about my shoulders, and my morion still on my head—for it served me well to be alert and full-armed at all times.

Now as I ate, I seemed to hear doors opening and closing stealthily in the back part of the tavern, and a low mumble of voices came to my ears. What this portended I knew not, but I was minded to finish my meal, and feigned to give no heed when the innkeeper, a silent, swarthy man in a leathern apron, came from some inner chamber, stared fixedly at me, and then departed again into the hinterlands of the tavern.

It was not long after his disappearance when another man entered the tavern from a side door—a small, hard-figured man with dark sharp features, somberly dressed, and wrapped in a black silk cloak. I felt his eyes upon me, but did not appear to regard him, except that I stealthily loosed my sword in its scabbard. He came hurriedly toward me, and hissed: "La Balafre!"

As he was obviously speaking to me, I turned, my hand on my hilt, and he gave back, his breath hissing through his teeth. So for an instant we faced each other. Then:

"Saint Denis! A woman! La Balafre, a *woman!* They did not tell me—I did not know—"

"Well?" I demanded warily, not understanding his bewilderment, but in no mind to let him know it.

"Well, it's no matter," he said at last. "You are not the first woman to wear breeches and a sword. Little matter what sort of a finger pulls the trigger, the ball speeds to the mark. Your master bade me watch for your cloak—it was by the gold thread that I recognized you. Come, come, it grows late. They await you in the secret room."

Now I realized that this man had mistaken me for the bravo I had slain; doubtless the fellow had been on his way to a tryst for some crime. I knew not what to say. If I denied that I was La Balafre, it was not likely his friends would allow me to go in peace without explaining how I came by his cloak. I saw no way out except to strike down the dark-faced man, and ride for my life. But with his next words, the whole situation changed.

"Put on your mask and wrap well your cloak about

you." he said. "None knows you here but I, and I only because that cloak was described to me. It was foolish of you to sit here openly in the tavern where any man might have seen you. The task we have to do is of such nature that all our identities must be hidden, not only tonight but henceforward. You know me only as Jehan. You will know none of the others, or they you."

Now at these words a mad whim seized me, born of recklessness and womanish curiosity. Saying naught, I rose, put on the mask I had found on the body of the real La Balafre, wrapped my cloak about me so that none could have known me for a woman, and followed the man who called himself Jehan.

He led the way through a door at the back of the room, which he closed and bolted behind us, and drawing forth a black mask similar to mine, he donned it. Then, taking a candle from a table, he led on down a narrow corridor with heavy oaken panels. At last he halted, extinguished the candle, and rapped cautiously on the wall. There was a fumbling on the other side, and a dim light glimmered through as a false panel was slid aside. Motioning me to follow him, Jehan glided through the opening, and after I had entered, closed it behind us.

I found myself in a small chamber, without visible doors or windows, though there must have been some subtle system of ventilation. A hooded lanthorn lit the room with a vague and ghostly light. Nine figures huddled against the walls on settles—nine figures wrapped closely in dark cloaks, feathered hats or black morions pulled low to meet the black masks which hid their faces. Only their eyes burned through the holes in the masks. None moved nor spake. It was like a conclave of the damned.

Jehan did not speak, but motioned me to take my place on a settle, and then he glided across the chamber and drew back another panel. Through this opening stalked another figure, masked and cloaked like the rest, but with a subtle different bearing. He strode like a man accustomed to command, and even in his disguise, there was something faintly familiar to me about him.

He stalked to the center of the small chamber, and Jehan motioned toward us on the settles, as if to say that all was in readiness. The tall stranger nodded and said: "You received your instructions before you came here. You know, all of you, that you have but to follow me, and obey my commands. Ask no questions; you are being well paid; that is sufficient for you to know. Speak as little as possible. You do not know me, and I do not know you. The less each man knows of his mates, the better for all. As soon as our task is completed, we scatter, each man for himself. Is that understood?"

Ten hooded heads wagged grimly in the lanthorn light. But I drew back on my settle, gathering my cloak more closely about me; he was understood better than he knew. I had heard that voice, under circumstances I was not likely to forget; it was the voice that had shouted commands to the murderers of Guiscard de Clisson, as I lay wounded in a cleft of the cliff and fought them off with my pistols. The man who commanded these villains amongst whom I had fallen was Renault d'Valence, the man who sought my life.

As his steely eyes, burning from his mask, swept over us, I unconsciously tensed myself, gripping my hilt beneath my cloak. But he could not recognize me in my disguise, were he Satan himself.

Motioning to Jehan, mine enemy arose and made toward the panel through which he had entered. Jehan beckoned us, and we followed d'Valence through the opening single file, a train of silent black ghosts. Behind us Jehan extinguished the lanthorn, and followed us. We groped our way through utter darkness for a short space, then a door swung open, and the broad shoulders of our leader were framed for an instant against the stars. We came out into a small courtyard behind the inn, where twelve horses champed restlessly and pawed the ground. Mine was among them, though I had told the servant to stable him. Evidently everyone in the tavern of the Half Moon had his orders.

Without a word we mounted and followed d'Valence across the court, and out into a path which led through the forest. We rode in silence, save for the clop of the hoofs on the hard soil, and the occasional creak of leather or clank of harness. We were headed westward, toward the coast, and presently the forest thinned to brush and scattered trees, and the path dwindled and vanished in a bushy maze. Here we rode no longer single file, but in a ragged clump. And I believed my opportunity had come. Whither we were riding I knew not, nor greatly cared. It must be some work of the Duc d'Alencon, since his right-hand man d'Valence was in command. But I did know that as long as d'Valence lived, neither my life nor the life of Etienne Villiers was worth a piece of broken copper.

It was dark; the moon had not yet risen, and the stars were hidden by rolling masses of clouds, which, though neither stormy nor very black, yet blotted out the light of the heavens in their ceaseless surging from horizon to horizon. We were not following any road, but rising through the wilderness. A night wind moaned through the trees, as I edged my horse closer and closer to that of Renault d'Valence, gripping my poniard beneath my cloak.

Now I was drawing up beside him, and heard him mutter to Jehan who rode knee to knee with him, "He was a fool to flout her, when she could have made him greater than the king of France. If Roger Hawksly—"

Rising in my stirrups I drove my poniard between his shoulders with all the strength of sinews nerved to desperate work. The breath went out of him in a gasp, and he pitched headlong from the saddle, and in that instant I wrenched my horse about and struck the spurs deep.

With a desperate heave and plunge he tore headlong through the shapes that hemmed us in, knocking steeds and riders aside, plunged through the bushes and was gone while they groped for their blades.

Behind me I heard startled oaths and yells, and the clank of steel, Jehan's voice yelling curses, and d'Valence's, choking and gasping, croaking orders. I cursed my luck. Even with the impact of the blow, I had known I had failed. D'Valence wore a shirt of chain mail under his doublet, even as I did. The poniard had bent almost double on it, without wounding him. It was only the terrific force of the blow which had knocked him, half stunned, from his steed. And knowing the man as I did, I knew that it was very likely he would quickly be upon my trail, unless his other business be too urgent to permit it—and urgent indeed would be the business that would interfere with d'Valence's private vengeance. Besides, if Jehan told him that "La Balafre" was a red-headed girl, he would be sure to recognize his old enemy, Agnes de Chastillon.

So I gave the horse the rein and rode at a reckless gallop over bushy expanses and through scattered woodlands, expecting each moment to hear the drum of hoofs behind me. I rode southward, toward the road where I was to meet Etienne Villiers, and came upon it more suddenly that I expected. The road ran westward to the coast, and we had been paralleling its course.

Perhaps a mile to the west stood a roadside cross of stone, where the road split, one branch running west and the other southwest, and it was there that I was to meet

Etienne Villiers. It lacked some hours till midnight, and I was not minded to wait in open view until he came, lest d'Valence come first. So when I came to the cross, I took refuge among the trees, which grew there in a dense clump, and set myself to wait for my companion.

The night was still, and I heard no sounds of pursuit; I hoped that if the bravos had pursued me, they had lost me in the darkness, which had been easy enough to do.

I tied my horse back among the trees, and hardly had I squatted among the shadows at the roadside when I heard the drumming of hoofs. But this noise came from the southwest, and was but a single horse. I crouched there, sword in hand, as the drumming grew louder and nearer, and presently the rising moon, peeping through the rolling clouds, disclosed a horseman galloping along the white road, his cloak billowing out behind him. And I recognized the lithe figure and feathered cap of Etienne Villiers.

How a King's Mistress Knelt to Me

HE PULLED up at the cross, and swore beneath his breath, speaking softly aloud to himself, as was his custom: "Too early, by hours; well, I'll await her here."

"You'll not have long to wait," said I, stepping from the shadows.

He wheeled in his saddle, pistol in hand, then laughed and swung down to earth.

"By Saint Denis, Agnes," said he, "I should never be surprised to find you anywhere, at any time. What, a horse? And no crow-bait, either! And a fine new cloak! By Satan, comrade, you have had luck—was it dice or the sword?"

"The sword," I answered.

"But why are you here so early?" he asked. "What portends this?"

"That Renault d'Valence is not far from us," I

73

answered, and heard his breath hiss between his teeth, saw his hand lock again on his pistol butt. So quickly I told him what had passed, and he shook his head.

"The Devil takes care of his own," he muttered. "Renault is hard to kill. But listen, I have a strange tale to tell, and until it is told, this is as good a place as another. Here we can watch and listen, and death cannot steal upon us behind closed doors and through secret corridors. And when my tale is told, we must take counsel as to our next move, because we can no longer count on Roger Hawksly.

"Listen: last night, just at moonrise, I approached the small isolated bay in which I knew the Englishman lay at anchor. We rogues have ways of learning secrets, as you know, Agnes. The coast thereabouts is rugged, with cliffs and headlands and inlets. The bay in question is surrounded by trees which grow down rugged slopes to the very edge of the water. I crept through them, and saw his ship, *The Resolute Friend*, lying at anchor, true enough, and all on board her apparently in drunken sleep. These pirates be fools, especially the English, who keep vile watch. I could see men stretched on the deck, with broken casks near them, and judged that those who were supposed to keep watch, had drunken themselves into helplessness.

"Now as I meditated whether to hail them, or to swim out to the ship, I heard the sound of muffled oars, and saw three longboats round the headland and sweep down on the silent ship. The boats were packed with men, and I saw the glint of steel in the moon. All unseen by the sleeping pirates, they drew up alongside, and I knew not whether to shout or be still, for I thought it might be Roger and his men returning from some raid.

"In the moonlight I saw them swarming up the chains—Englishmen, beyond doubt, dressed in the garb of common sailors. Then as I watched, one of the drunkards on deck stirred in his sleep, gaped, and then suddenly scrambled up, screaming a warning. Up out of the hold and out of the cabin rushed Roger Hawksly and his men, in their shirts, half asleep, grasping their weapons in bewilderment, and over the rail swarmed these newcomers, who fell on the pirates sword in hand.

"It was a massacre rather than a fight. The pirates, half asleep and evidently half drunk as well, were cut down, almost to a man. I saw their bodies hurled overboard. Some few leaped into the water and swam ashore, but most died.

"Then the victors hauled up the anchor, and some of them returning into the boats, towed *The Resolute Friend* out of the inlet, and watching from where I lay, I presently saw her spread her sails and stand out to sea. Presently another ship rounded the headland and followed her.

"Of the survivors of the pirate crew I know nothing, for they fled into the woods and vanished. But Roger Hawksly is no longer master of a ship, and whether he lives or died, I know not, but we must find another man who will take us to Italy.

"But herein is a mystery: some of the Englishmen who took *The Resolute Friend* were but rough seamen. But others were not. I understand English; I know a high-born voice when I hear it, and tarry breeches cannot always conceal rank from a sharp eye. The moon was bright as day. Agnes, those seamen were led by noblemen disguised in mean apparel."

"Why?" I wondered.

"Aye, why! 'Tis easy to see how the trick was done. They sailed up to the headland, where they anchored, out of sight from the inlet, and sent men in boats to take their prey. But why take such a desperate chance? Luck was on their side, else Hawksly and his sea-wolves had been sober and alert, and had blown them out of the water as they came on. There is but one solution: secrecy. That likewise explains the noblemen in seamen's shirts and breeks. For some reason someone wished to destroy the pirates swiftly, silently, and secretly. As to the reason for that, I do not know, since Hawksly was a man hated equally by the French and the English."

"Why, as to that—hark!"

Down the road, from the east, sounded the pound of racing hoofs. Clouds had rolled again over the moon, and it was dark as Erebus.

"D'Valence!" I hissed. "He is following me—and alone. Give me a pistol! He will not escape this time!"

"We had best be sure he is alone," expostulated Etienne as he handed me a pistol.

"He's alone," I snarled. " 'Tis but one rider—but if the Devil himself rode with him—*ha*!"

A flying shape loomed out of the night; at that instant a single moonbeam cut through the clouds and faintly illumined the racing horse and its rider. And I fired pointblank.

The great horse reared and plunged headlong, and a piteous cry cut the night. It was echoed by Etienne. He had seen, as had I, in the flash of the shot, a woman clinging to the reins of the flying steed.

We ran forward, seeing a slender figure stirring on the ground beside the steed—a figure which knelt and lifted helpless arms, whimpering in fright.

"Are you hurt?" gasped Etienne. "My God, Agnes, you've killed a woman—"

"I struck the horse," I answered. "He threw up his head just as I fired. Here, let me see to her!"

Bending over her, I lifted her face, a pallid oval in the darkness. Under my hard fingers her garments and flesh felt soft and wondrous fine.

"Are you hurt badly, wench?" I demanded.

But at the sound of my voice she gave a gasping cry and threw her arms about my knees.

"Oh, you too are a woman! Have mercy! Do not hurt me! Please—"

"Cease these whimperings, wench," I ordered impatiently. "Here is naught to hurt you. Are your bones broken by reason of the fall?"

"Nay, I am only bruised and shaken. But, oh, my poor horse—"

"I'm sorry," I muttered. "I do not slay animals willingly. I was aiming at his rider."

"But why should you murder me?" she wailed. "I know you not—"

"I am Agnes de Chastillon," I answered, "whom some men call Dark Agnes de La Fere. Who are you?"

I had lifted her to her feet and released her, and now as she stood before us, the moon brake suddenly through the clouds and flooded the road with silvery light. I looked in amaze at the richness of our captive's garments, and the beauty of her oval face, framed in a glory of hair that was like dark foam; her dark eyes glowed like black jewels in the moonlight. And from Etienne came a strangled cry.

"My lady!" He doffed his feathered cap, and dropped to his knee. "Kneel, Agnes, kneel, girl! It is Francoise de Foix!"

"Why should an honest woman kneel to a royal strumpet?" I demanded, thrusting my thumbs into my girdle and bracing my legs wide as I faced her.

Etienne was stricken dumb, and the girl seemed to wince at my peasant candor.

"Rise, I beg of you," she said humbly to Etienne, and he did so, cap in hand.

"But this was most unwise, my lady!" said he. "To have come alone and at night—"

"Oh," she cried suddenly, catching at her temples, as if reminded of her mission. "Even now they may be slaying him! Oh, sir, if you be a man, aid me!"

She seized Etienne by the doublet and shook him in the agony of her insistence.

"Listen," she begged, though Etienne was listening with all his ears. "I came here tonight, alone, as you see, to endeavor to right a wrong, and to save a life.

"You know me as Francoise de Foix, the mistress of the king—"

"I have seen you at court, where I was not always a stranger," said Etienne, speaking with a strange difficulty. "I know you for the most beautiful woman in all France."

"I thank you, my friend," she said, still clinging to him. "But the world sees little of what goes on behind the palace doors. Men say I twist the king about my finger, God help me—but I swear I am but a pawn in a game I do not understand—the slave of a greater will than that of Francis."

"Louise of Savoy," muttered Etienne.

"Aye, who through me, rules her son, and through him, all France. It was she who made me what I am. Else I had been, not the mistress of a king, but the honest wife of some honest man.

"Listen, my friend, oh, listen and believe me! Tonight a man is riding toward the coast, and death! And the letter which lured him there was written by me! Oh, I am a hateful thing, to thus serve one who—who loves me—

"But I am not my own mistress. I am the slave of Louise of Savoy. What she bids me do, that I do, or else I smart for it. She dominates me and I dare not resist her. This—this man was in Alencon, when he received the letter begging him to meet me at a certain tavern near the coast. Only for me would he have gone, for he well knows of his powerful enemies. But me he trusts—oh, God pity me!"

She sobbed hysterically for an instant, while I watched in wonder, for I could never weep, my whole life.

"It is a plot of Louise," she said. "Once she loved this man, but he scorned her, and she plots his ruin. Already she has shorn him of titles and honor; now she would rob him of life itself.

"At the tavern of the Hawk he will be met, not by my miserable self, but by a band of hired bravos, who will slay his servants and take him captive and deliver him to the pirate Roger Hawksly, who has been paid well to dispose of him forever."

"Why so much planning and elaborate work?" I demanded. "Surely a dagger in the back would do the job as well."

"Not even Louise dares discovery," she answered. "The—the man is too powerful—"

"There is only one man in France whom Louise hates so fiercely," said Etienne, looking full into Francoise's eyes. She bowed her head, then lifted it and returned the look with her lustrous dark eyes.

"Aye!" she said simply.

"A blow to France," muttered Etienne, "if *he* should fail—but my lady, Roger Hawksly will not be there to receive him." And he swiftly related what he had seen on the coast.

"Then the bravos will slay him themselves," she said with a shudder. "They will never dare let him go. They are led by Jehan, the right hand man of Louise—"

"And by Renault d'Valence," muttered Etienne. "I see it all now; you were with that band, Agnes. I wonder if d'Alencon knows of the plot."

"No," answered Francoise. "But Louise plans to raise

him to the rank of her victim; so she uses his most trusted man, Renault d'Valence for her schemes. But, oh, we waste time! Please will you not aid me? Ride with me to the tavern of the Hawk. Perchance we may rescue him—may reach him in time to get him away before they arrive. I stole away, and have ridden all night at top speed—please, please aid me!"

"Francoise de Foix has never to ask twice of Etienne Villiers," said Etienne, in that strange unnatural voice, standing in the moonlight, cap in hand. Perhaps it was the moon, but a strange expression was on his face, softening the lines of cynicism and wild living, and making him seem another and nobler man.

"And you, mademoiselle!" The court beauty turned to me, with her arms outstretched. "You would not kneel to me, Dark Agnes; look, I kneel to you!"

And she so did—down in the dust on her knees, her white hands clasped and her dark eyes sparkling with tears.

"Get up, girl," I said awkwardly, ashamed for some obscure reason. "Kneel not to me. I'll do all I can. I know nothing of court intrigues and what you have said buzzes in my skull until I am dizzy, but what we can do, that we will do!"

With a sob she rose and threw both her soft arms about my neck and kissed me on the lips, so I was further ashamed. It was the first time I remembered anyone ever kissing me.

"Come," I said roughly. "We waste time."

Etienne lifted the girl into his saddle and swung up behind her, and I mounted the great black horse.

"What do you plan?" he asked me.

"I have no plan. We must be guided by the circumstances which confront us. Let us ride as swiftly as may be for the Inn of the Hawk. If Renault wasted much time in looking for me—as doubtless he did—he and his bravos may not yet have reached the tavern. If they have—well, we are but two swords, but we can but do our best."

And so I fell to recharging the pistol I had taken from Etienne, and a tedious task it was, in the darkness, and riding hard. So what speech passed between Etienne and Francoise de Foix I know not, but the murmur of their voices reached me from time to time, and in his voice was an unfamiliar softness—strange in a rogue like Etienne Villiers.

So we came at last upon the tavern of the Hawk, which loomed stark against the night, dark save for a single lanthorn in the common room. Silence reigned utterly, and there was the scent of fresh-spilled blood—

In the road before the tavern lay a man in the livery of a lackey, his white staring face turned to the stars, and dabbled with blood. Near the door lay a shape in a black cloak, and the fragments of a black mask, soaked in blood, lay beside it, with a feathered hat. But the features of the man were but a ghastly mask of hacked and slashed flesh, unrecognizable.

Just inside the door lay another lackey, his brains oozing from his crushed head, a broken sword still gripped in his hand. Inside the tavern was a waste of broken settles and smashed tables, with great gouts of blood fouling the floor. A third lackey lay huddled in the corner, his blood-stained doublet showing a dozen sword-thrusts. Over all hung silence like a pall.

Francoise had fallen with a moan when she saw the horror of it all, and now Etienne half led, half carried her in his arms.

"Renault and his cutthroats were here," he said. "They

have taken their prey and gone. But where? All the servants would have fled in terror, not to return until daylight."

But peering here and there, sword in hand, I saw something huddled under an over-turned settle, and dragging it forth, disclosed a terrified serving wench who fell on her knees and bawled for mercy. "Have done, jade," I said impatiently. "Here is none to harm you. But say quickly what has occurred."

"The men in masks," she whimpered. "They came suddenly in at the door—"

"Did you not hear their horses?" demanded Etienne.

"Would Renault warn his victim?" I asked impatiently. "Doubtless they left their steeds a short distance away and came softly on foot. Go on, girl,"

"They fell on the gentleman and his servants," she blubbered. "The gentleman who had arrived earlier this night and who sat silently at his wine, and seemed in doubt and meditation. As the masked men entered he sprang up and cried out that he was betrayed—"

"Oh!" It was a cry of agony from Francoise de Foix. She clasped her hands and writhed as in agony.

"Then there was fighting and slaying and death," wailed the wench. "They slew the gentleman's servants, and him they bound and dragged away—"

"Was it he who so disfigured the bravo who lies outside the door?" I demanded.

"Nay, he slew him with a pistol ball. The leader of the masks, the tall man who wore a chain-mail shirt under his doublet—he hacked the dead man's face with the sword—"

"Aye," I muttered. "D'Valence would not wish to leave him to be identified."

"And this same man, before he left, passed his sword through each of the dying lackeys to make sure they were dead," she sobbed in terror. "I hid under the settle and watched, for I was too frightened to run, as did the innkeeper and the other servants."

"In which direction did they go?" I demanded, shaking the wretched girl in my intensity.

"That—that way!" she gasped, pointing. "Down the old road to the coast."

"Did you overhear anything that might give a clue as to their destination?"

"No—no—they spoke little, and I so frightened."

"Hoofs of the devil, girl!" I exclaimed in a fury. "Such work is never done in silence. Think hard—remember something they said, before I turn you across my knee."

"All I remember," she gasped, "is that the tall leader said to the poor gentleman, once they had him bound—doffing his helmet in a sweeping bow—'My lord,' quoth he mockingly, 'your ship awaits you!'"

"Sure they would put him aboard ship," exclaimed Etienne. "And the nearest place a ship would put in is Corsair Cove! They cannot be far ahead of us. If they followed the old road—as they would be likely to do, not knowing the country as I do—it will take them half an hour longer to reach the cove than it will take us, following a short cut of which I know."

"Come then!" cried Francoise, revived anew by the hope of action. And a few moments later, we were riding through the shadows for the coast. We followed a dim path, its mouth hidden by dense bushes, which wound along a rocky ridge, descending seaward amid boulders and gnarled trees.

So we came into a cove, surrounded by rugged slopes, thickly treed, and through the trees we saw the glimmer of water, and the shimmer of the furtive moon on broad sails. And leaving our horses, and Francoise with them, we crept forward, Etienne and I, and presently looked out

upon an open beach, lighted by the moon which at the
time shone out through the curling clouds.

Under the shadows of the trees stood a group of black
and sombre figures, and out of a boat, just drawn up on
the beach (we could still see the foam floating on the water
that had swirled in her wake) trooped a score of men in
seamen's garb. Out in the deeper water rode a ship, the
moonlight glinting on her gilt-work and spreading
courses, and Etienne swore softly.

"That's *The Resolute Friend*, but those are not her
crew. *They* are food for the fishes. These are the men who
took her. What devil's game is this?"

We saw a man pushed forward by the masked
bravos—a man tall and well-formed, who, even in torn
shirt and blood-stained, with his arms bound behind him,
had the bearing of a leader among men.

"Saint Denis," breathed Etienne. "It is he, right
enough."

"Who?" I demanded. "Who is this fellow we must risk
our lives to rescue?"

"Charles," he began, then broke off: "Listen!"

We had wriggled nearer, and Renault d'Valence's voice
came plainly to us.

"Nay, that was not in the bargain. I know you not. Let
Roger Hawksly, your captain, come ashore. I wish to be
sure he knows his instructions."

"Captain Hawksly cannot be disturbed," answered one
of the seamen in accented French; he was a tall man who
bore himself proudly. "There is no need to fear; yonder is
The Resolute Friend; here are Hawksly's bullies. You
have given us the prisoner. We will take him aboard and
set sail. You have done your part; now we will do ours."

I was staring in fascination, having never seen
Englishmen before. These were all tall men and stalwart,
with goodly swords buckled at their hips, and steel

glinting under their doublets. Never saw I such proud-seeming sailormen, or seamen so well armed. They had seized the man Etienne called Charles, and were hauling him to the boat—which task seemed to be supervised by a tall portly man in a red cloak.

"Aye," said Renault, "yonder lies *The Resolute Friend*; I know her well, or I had never delivered my prisoner to you. But I know you not. Call Captain Hawksly, or I take my prisoner back again."

"Enough!" exclaimed the other arrogantly. "I tell you Hawksly cannot come. You do not know me—"

But d'Valence, who had been listening closely to the other's voice, cried out sharply and fiercely.

"Nay, by God, I think I *do* know you, my lord!" And knocking off the seaman's bonnet the man wore, he disclosed a steel cap beneath, crowning a proud hawk-like face.

"So!" exclaimed d'Valence. "You would take my prisoner—but not to slay—nay, to hold as a club over the head of Francis! Rogue I may be, but traitor to my king—never!"

And snatching forth a pistol he fired point-blank, not at the lord, but at the prisoner Charles.

But the Englishman knocked up his arm, and the ball went wide.

The next instant all was turmoil and confusion as Renault's bravos rushed in in response to his shouts, and the Englishmen met them hand to hand. I saw the blades glimmer and flash in the moonlight as Renault and the English lord fought, and suddenly Renault's sword was dyed red and the Englishman was down, gasping out his life on the sand.

Now I saw that the men who had been hauling along the prisoner Charles had hastened into the fray, leaving him in the hands of the portly man in the red cloak who was dragging him, despite his struggles, toward the boat drawn up on the beach. Now I heard the clack of oarlocks, and looking toward the ship, saw three other boats putting towards shore.

But even as I looked, I was whispering to Etienne, and we broke cover and ran silently across the stretch of white sand, toward the struggling pair near the beach. All about us raged the fight as the bravos, outnumbered but dangerous as wolves, slashed and parried and thrust with the reckless Englishmen.

Even as we came into the fray, an Englishman rushed at each of us. Etienne fired and missed—for moonlight is deceptive—and the next instant was fighting sword to sword. I did not fire until my muzzle almost touched my enemy's bosom, and when I pulled the trigger, the heavy ball tore through the chain-mail beneath his doublet like paper, and the lifted sword fell harmless into the sand.

A few more strides brought me up with Charles and his captor, but even as I reached them, one was before me. While men fought and slew and cursed madly, d'Valence had never lost sight of his objective. Realizing that he could not retake his prisoner, he was determined on slaying him.

Now he had cut his way through the melee, and ran with grim purpose across the sands, his sword dripping in his hand. Running up to the prisoner, he cut murderously at his unprotected head. The stroke was parried, awkwardly, by the portly man in the red cloak, who began bawling for aid in a gasping, short-winded voice which went unheeded in the uproar of the melee. So ineptly had he parried that the sword was beaten out of his hand. But before d'Valence could strike again, I came silently and swiftly up from the side, and thrust at him with all my strength, meaning to spit him through the neck, above the gorget. But again luck betrayed me; my foot slipped in the sand, and the point rasped harmlessly along his mail.

Instantly he turned and recognized me. He had lost his mask, and his eyes danced with a sort of reckless madness in the moonlight.

"By God!" he cried, with a wild laugh. "It is the red-haired sword-wench!"

Even as he spoke he parried my whistling blade, and with no further words, we set to work, slashing and thrusting. He drew blood from my sword-hand, and from my thigh, but I smote him with such fury that my edge bit through his morion and into the scalp beneath, so that blood ran from under his burganet and trickled down his face. Another such stroke had finished him, but he, casting a quick glance aside, saw that most of his bravos were down, and he in desperate case. So with another wild laugh he bounded back, sprang aside, cut his way through those who sought to stay him, with half a dozen flailing strokes, and bounding clear, vanished in the shadows, whence presently emerged the sound of a running horse.

Now I whirled quickly to the prisoner, whose arm the portly man in red still gripped, puffing and panting, and slashing the cords that bound his arms, I thrust him toward the woods. But so wrought up was I that my push was more powerful than I intended, and sent him sprawling on all-fours.

The man in the red cloak squalled wildly and sprang to seize his captive again, but I buffeted him aside, and dragging Charles to his feet, bade him run. But he seemed half dazed by a chance blow of the flat of a blade on the pate. But now Etienne, his sword dripping red, ran forward and seizing the captive's arm, urged him toward the woods.

And the man in the red cloak, evidently in desperation

resorted to the tactics of d'Valence, for catching up his sword, he ran at the back of Charles and hewed at him. But even as he did so, I smote him under the armpit with such power that he rolled in the sand, screaming like a stuck pig. Now divers of the English halted in their rush towards me, and shouted in horror and ran to pick up the fellow; for some of the links of his chain shirt had parted under my edge, and he had ben wounded slightly, so that the blood oozed through his doublet.

They shouted a name that sounded like "Wolsey," and halted in their pursuit to lift him and see to his wound, while he cursed at them. And Etienne and I bore the rescued man between us into the woods, and to the horses where Francoise awaited us.

She stood like a white shadow under the moon-dappled trees, and when he saw her, he gave back with an exclamation.

"Oh, Charles," she exclaimed, "have pity! I had no choice—"

"I trusted you above all others," said he, more in sadness than anger.

"My Lord Duc of Bourbon," said Etienne, touching his shoulder, "it is my privilege to tell you that what wrong has been done, has been righted this night as well as might be. If Francoise de Foix betrayed you, she has risked her life to rescue you. Now I beg of you, take these horses and ride, for none knows what next may chance to befall. That was Cardinal Wolsey who led those men, and he in not easy to defeat."

Like a man in a dream the Duke of Bourbon mounted, and Etienne lifted Francoise de Foix up into the other saddle. They reined away and rode through the moonlight and so vanished. And I turned to Etienne.

"Well," said I, "with all our chivalry, here are we back

where we began, without money, or means of reaching Italy; nay, you have even given away your horse! What shall be our next adventure?"

"I held Francoise de Foix in my arms," he answered. "After that, any adventure is but anticlimax for Etienne Villiers."

MISTRESS OF DEATH*

* with Gerald W. Page

AHEAD OF me in the dark alley, steel clashed and a man cried out as men cry only when death-stricken. Around a corner of the winding way three mantled shapes came running, blindly, as men run in panic and terror. I drew back against the wall to let them go past, and two crowded by me without even seeing me, breathing in hysterical gasps; but the third, running with his chin on his shoulder, blundered full against me.

He shrieked like a damned soul, and evidently deeming himself attacked, grappled me wildly, tearing at me with his teeth like a mad dog. With a curse I broke his grasp and flung him from me against the wall, but the violence of my exertion caused my foot to slip in a puddle on the stones, and I stumbled and went to my knee.

He fled screaming on up the alley, but as I rose, a tall figure loomed above me, like a phantom out of the deeper

shadows. The light of a distant cresset gleamed dully on
his morion and the sword lifted above my head. I barely
had time to parry the stroke; the sparks flew as our steel
met, and I returned the stroke with a thrust of such
violence that my point drove through teeth and neck and
rang against the lining of his steel head-piece.

Who my attackers were I knew not, but there was no
time for parley or explanation. Dim figures were upon me
in the semi-darkness and blades whickered about my
head. A stroke that clanged full upon my morion filled my
eyes with sparks of fire, and abandoning the point in my
extremity, I hewed right and left and heard men grunt and
curse as my sword's edge gashed them. Then, as I stepped
back to avoid a swiping cut, my foot caught in the cloak of
the man I had killed, and I fell sprawling over the corpse.

There was a fierce cry of triumph, and one sprang
forward, sword lifted—but ere he could strike or I could
lift my blade above my head, a quick step sounded behind
me, a dim figure loomed in the uncertain light, and the
downward sweeping blade rang on a sword in mid-air.

"Dog!" quoth the stranger with curious accent. "Will
you strike a fallen man?"

The other roared and cut at him madly, but by that
time I was on my feet again, and as the others pressed in, I
met them with point and edge, thrusting and slashing like
a demon, for I was wild with fury at having been in such a
plight as the stranger rescued me from. A side-long glance
showed me the latter driving his sword through the body
of the man who opposed him, and at this, and as I pressed
them, drawing blood at each stroke, the rogues gave way
and fled fleetly down the alley.

I turned then to my unknown friend, and saw a lithe,
compactly-built man but little taller than myself. The
glare of the distant cresset fell dimly upon him, and I saw
that he was clad in fine Cordovan boots and velvet

doublet, beneath which I glimpsed a glint of fine mesh-mail. A fine crimson cloak was flung over his shoulder, a feathered cap on his head, and beneath this his eyes, cold and light, danced restlessly. His face was clean-shaven and brown, with high cheekbones and thin lips, and there were scars that hinted of an adventurous career. He bore himself with something of a swagger, and his every action betokened steelspring muscles and the coordination of a swordsman.

"I thank you, my friend," quoth I. "Well for me that you came at the moment which you did."

"Zounds!" cried he. "Think naught of it. 'Twas no more than I'd have done for any man—but, Saint Andrew! You're a woman!"

There being no reply to that, I cleaned my blade and sheathed it, while he gaped at me openmouthed.

"Agnes de la Fere!" he said slowly, at length. "It can be no other. I have heard of you, even in Scotland. Your hand, girl! I have yearned to meet you. Nor is it an unworthy thing even for Dark Agnes to shake the hand of John Stuart."

I grasped his hand, though in sooth, I had never heard of him, feeling steely thews in his fingers and a quick nervous grip that told me of a passionate, hair-trigger nature.

"Who were these rogues who sought your life?" he asked.

"I have many enemies," I answered, "but I think these were mere skulking rogues, robbers and murderers. They were pursuing three men, and I think tried to cut my throat to hush my tongue."

"Likely enough," quoth he. "I saw three men in black mantles flee out of the alley mouth as though Satan were at their heels, which aroused my curiosity, so I came to see what was forward, especially as I heard the rattle of steel.

Saint Andrew! Men said your sword-play was like summer lightning, and it is even as they said! But let us see if the rogues have indeed fled or are merely lurking beyond that crook to stab us in the back as we depart."

He stepped cautiously around the crook and swore under his breath.

"They are gone, in sooth, but I see something lying in the alley. I think it is a dead man."

Then I remembered the cry I heard, and I joined him. A few moments later we were bending over two forms that lay sprawled in the mud of the alley. One was a small man, mantled like the three who had fled, but with a deep gash in his breast that had let out his life. But as I spoke to Stuart on the matter, he swore suddenly. He had turned the other man on his back, and was staring at him in surprise.

"This man has been dead for hours," quoth he. "Moreover he died not by sword or pistol. Look! It is the mark of the gallows! And he is clad still in the gibbet-shirt. By Saint Andrew, Agnes, do you know who this is?" And when I shook my head, "It is Costranno, the Italian sorcerer, who was hanged at dawn this morning on the gibbet outside the walls, for practicing the black arts. He it was who poisoned the son of the Duke of Tours and caused the blame to be laid upon an innocent man. But Francoise de Bretagny, suspecting the truth, trapped him into a confession to her, and laid the facts before the authorities."

"I heard something of this matter," quoth I. "But I have been in Chartres only a matter of a week."

"It is Costranno, well enough," said Stuart, shaking his head. "His features are so distorted I would not have known him, save that the middle finger of his left hand is missing. And this other is Jacques Pelligny, his pupil in the black arts. Sentence of death was passed on him,

likewise, but he had fled and could not be found. Well, his
art did not save him from a footpad's sword. Costranno's
followers have cut him down from the gibbet—but why
should they have brought the body back into the city?"

"There is something in Pelligny's hand," I said, prying
the dead fingers apart. It was as if, even in death, they
gripped what they held. It was a fragment of gold chain,
and fastened to it a most curious red jewel that gleamed in
the darkness like an angry eye.

"Saint Andrew!" muttered Stuart. "A rare stone, i'
faith—hark!" he started to his feet. "The watch! We must
not be found by these corpses!"

Far down the alley I saw the glow of moving lanthorns
and heard the tramp of mailed feet. As I scrambled up, the
jewel and chain slipped from my fingers—it was almost as
if they were snatched from my hand—and fell full on the
breast of the dead sorcerer. I did not wish to take the time
to retrieve it, so I hurried up the alley after Stuart, and
glancing back, I saw the jewel glittering like a crimson star
on the dead man's bosom.

Emerging from the alley into a narrow winding street,
scarcely better lighted, we hurried along it until we came
to an inn, and entered it. Then, seating ourselves at a table
somewhat apart from the others who wrangled and cast
dice on the wine-stained boards, we called for wine and
the host brought us two great jacks.

"To our better acquaintance," quoth John Stuart,
lifting his tankard. "By Saint Andrew, now that I see you
in the light, I admire you the more. You are a fine, tall
woman, but even in morion, doublet, trunk-hose and
boots, none could mistake you for a man. Well are you
called Dark Agnes! For all your red hair and fair skin
there is something strange and dark about you. Men say
you move through life like one of the Fates, unmoved,
unchangeable, potent with tragedy and doom, and that

the men who ride with you do not live long. Tell me, girl, why did you don breeks and take the road of men?"

I shook my head, unable to say myself, but as he urged me to tell him something of myself, I said, "My name is Agnes de Chastillon, and I was born in the village of La Fere, in Normandy. My father is the bastard son of the Duc de Chastillon and a peasant woman—a mercenary soldier of the Free Companies until he grew too old to march and fight. If I had not been tougher than most he would have killed me with his beating before I was grown. When at last he sought to marry me to a man I hated, I killed that man, and fled from the village. One Etienne Villiers befriended me, but also taught me that a helpless woman is fair prey to all men, and when I bested him in even fight, I learned that I was as strong as most men, and quicker.

"Later I fell in with Guiscard de Clisson, a leader of the Free Companies, who taught me the use of the sword before he was slain in an ambush. I took naturally to the life of a man, and can drink, swear, march, fight and boast with the best of them. I have yet to meet my equal at sword play."

Stuart scowled slightly as if my word did not please him overmuch, and he lifted his tankard, quaffed deeply, and said, "There be as good men in Scotland as in France, and there men say that John Stuart's blade is not made of straw. But who is this?"

The door had opened and a gust of cold wind made the candles flicker, and sent a shiver over the men on the settles. A tall man entered, closing the door behind him. He was wrapped in a wide black mantle, and when he raised his head and his glance roved over the tavern, a silence fell suddenly. That face was strange and unnatural in appearance, being so dark in hue that it was almost black. His eyes were strange, murky and staring. I saw several topers cross themselves as they met his gaze, and then he seated himself at a table in a corner furthest from the candles, and drew his mantle closer about him, though the night was warm. He took the tankard proffered him by an apprehensive slattern and bent his head over it, so his face was no longer visible under his slouch hat, and the hum of the tavern began again, though somewhat subdued.

"Blood on that mantle," said John Stuart. "If that man be not a cutthroat, then I am much befooled. Host, another bottle!"

"You are the first Scotsman I ever met," said I, "though I have had dealings with Englishmen."

"A curse on the breed!" he cried. "The devil take them all into his keeping! And a curse on my enemies who exiled me from Scotland."

"You are an exile?" I asked.

"Aye! With scant gold in my sporran. But fortune ever favors the brave." And he laid hand on the hilt at his hip.

But I was watching the stranger in the corner, and Stuart turned to stare at him. The man had lifted his hand and crooked a finger at the fat host, and that rogue drew nigh, wiping his hands on his leathern apron and uneasy in his expression. There was something about the black mantled stranger that repelled men.

The stranger spoke, but his words were a mumble and mine host shook his head in the bewilderment.

"An Italian," muttered Stuart. "I know that jabber anywhere."

But the stranger shifted into French and as he spoke, haltingly, his words grew plainer, his voice fuller.

"Francoise de Bretagny," quoth he, and repeated the name several times. "Where is the house of Francoise de Bretagny?"

The inn-keeper began giving him directions, and

Stuart muttered: "Why should that ill-visaged Italian rogue desire to go to Francoise de Bretagny?"

"From what I hear," I answered cynically, "it is no great surprise to hear any man asking for her house."

"Lies are always told about beautiful women," answered Stuart, lifting his tankard. "Because she is said to be the mistress of the Duc of Orleans does not mean that she—"

He froze suddenly, tankard to lip, staring, and I saw an expression of surprise pass over his brown, scarred face. At that moment the Italian had risen, and drawing his wide mantle about him, made for the door.

"Stop him!" roared Stuart, leaping to his feet, and dragging out his sword. "Stop that rogue!"

But at that instant a band of soldiers in morions and breastplates came shouldering in, and the Italian glided out past them and shut the door behind him. Stuart started forward with a curse, to halt as the soldiers barred the way. Striding into the center of the tavern, and roving a stern glance over all the cringing occupants, the captain, a tall man in a gleaming breastplate, said loudly: "Agnes de La Fere, I arrest you for the murder of Jacques Pelligny!"

"What do you mean, Tristan?" I exclaimed angrily, springing up. "I did not kill Pelligny!"

"This woman saw you leave the alley where the man was slain," answered he, indicating a tall, fair wench in feathers and beads who cowered in the grasp of a burly man-at-arms and would not meet my gaze. I knew her well, a courtesan whom I had befriended, and whom I would not have expected to give false testimony against me.

"Then she must have seen me too," quoth John Stuart, "for I was with Agnes. If you arrest her you must arrest me too, and by Saint Andrew, my sword will have something to say about that."

"I have naught to do with you," answered Tristan. "My business is with this woman."

"Man, you are a fool," cried Stuart gustily. "She did not kill Pelligny. And what if she did? Was not the rogue under sentence of death?"

"He was meat for the hangman, not the private citizen," answered Tristan.

"Listen," said Stuart. "He was slain by footpads, who then attacked Agnes who chanced to be traversing the alley at the time. I came to her aid, and we slew two of the rogues. Did you not find their bodies, with masks to their heads to prove their trades?"

"We saw no such thing," answered Tristan. "Nor were you seen thereabouts, so your testimony is without value. This woman here saw Agnes de La Fere pursue Pelligny into the alley and there stab him. So I am forced to take her to the prison."

"I know well why you wish to arrest me, Tristan," I said coldly, approaching him with an easy tread. "I had not been to Chartres a day before you sought to make me your mistress. Now you take this revenge upon me. Fool! I am mistress only to Death!"

"Enough of this idle talk," ordered Tristan curtly. "Seize her, men!" It was his last command on earth, for my sword was through him before he could lift his hand. The guard closed in on me with a yell, and as I thrust and parried, John Stuart sprang to my side and in an instant the inn was a madhouse, with stamping boots, clanging blades and the curses and yells of slaughter. Then we broke through, leaving the floor strewn with corpses, and gained the street. As we broke through the door I saw the wench they brought to testify against me cowering behind an overturned settle and I grasped her thick yellow locks and dragged her with me into the street.

"Down that alley," gasped John Stuart. "Other guardsmen will be here anon. Saint Andrew, Agnes, will you burden yourself with that big hussy? We must take to our heels!"

"I have a score to settle with her," I gritted, for all my hot blood was roused. I hauled her along with us until we made a turn in the alley and halted for breath.

"Watch the street," I bade him, and then turning to the cowering wench, I said in calm fury: "Margot, if an open enemy deserves a thrust of steel, what fate does a traitress deserve? Not four days agone I saved you from a beating at the hands of a drunken soldier, and gave you money because your tears touched my foolish compassion. By Saint Trignan, I have a mind to cut the head from your fair shoulders!"

"Oh, Agnes," she sobbed, falling to her knees, and clasping my legs. "Have mercy, I—"

"I'll spare your worthless life," I said angrily, beginning to unsling my sword belt. "But I mean to turn up your petticoats and whip you as no beadle ever did."

"Nay, Agnes!" she wailed. "First hear me! I did not lie! It is true that I saw you and the Scotsman coming from the alley with naked swords in your hands. But the watch said merely that three bodies were lying in the alley, and two were masked, showing they were thieves. Tristan said whoever slew them did a good night's work, and asked me if I had seen any coming from the alley. So I thought no harm, and replied that I saw you and the Scotsman John Stuart. But when I spoke your name, he smiled and told his men that he had his reasons for desiring to get Agnes de La Fere in a dungeon, helpless and unarmed, and bade them do as he told them. So he told me that my testimony about you would be accepted, but the rest, about John

Stuart, and the two thieves, he would not accept. And he threatened me so terribly that I dared not defy him."

"The foul dog," I muttered. "Well, there is a new captain of the watch in hell tonight."

"But you said *three* bodies," broke in John Stuart. "Were there not four? Pelligny, two thieves, and the body of Costranno?"

She shook her head.

"I saw the bodies. There were but three. Pelligny lay deep in the alley, fully clad, the other two around the crook, and the larger was naked."

"Eh?" ejaculated Stuart. "By Heaven, that Italian! I have but now remembered! On, to the house of Francoise de Bretagny!"

"Why there?" I demanded.

"When the Italian in the inn drew his cloak about him to depart," answered Stuart, "I glimpsed on his breast a fragment of golden chain and a great red jewel—I believe the very jewel Pelligny grasped in his hand when we found him. I believe that man is a friend of Costranno's, a magician come to take vengeance on Francoise de Bretagny! Come!"

He set impetuously off up the alley, and I followed him, while the girl Margot scurried away in another direction, evidently glad to get off with a whole skin.

Stuart led the way, grimly silent, and I followed after him, somewhat perplexed by his silence and the silence of the street. For strangely silent were the dark, twisting streets, silent even for night. Involuntarily, I shuddered, though whether at the silence of the cold, I could not say. We encountered no one, not even soldiers, on our way to the home of Francoise de Bretagny.

It was not far to her home from the tavern where we fled the watch, though the tavern lay huddled among the squalor of the town's least reputable quarter and the home of Francoise de Bretagny, as befitted so magnificent a structure, was in a neighborhood suitable to the wealthiest noblewoman. No lights shone in the windows as we approached, and indeed none of the neighbor houses were lit at this time of night. We paused, John Stuart and I, without the courtyard gate and strained our ears, but the silence beat on us like the darkness, oppressive and threatening.

It was John Stuart who reached forward and pushed the gate, which opened noiselessly at his touch.

"Ah!" said he a moment later. "The lock's been broken and within the half hour, I'll wager."

"Inside, then," I replied, barely able to keep my voice to a whisper. "Even now we may be too late!"

"Aye," Stuart said, shoving the gate open the rest of the way. I heard the rasp of steel against scabbard as he drew his sword, and the dark shadow that was John Stuart's form moved agilely through the gate and I followed after. Within the courtyard it was as still as it was without, but there were thicker shadows here, for around us grew trees and thick shrubbery, as still as dark statues in the breeze-calmed night!

"Saint Andrew!" I heard John Stuart exclaim, and saw the dark form of his body bend and crouch to the ground, bending over something—or someone. I moved to his side and peered down.

It was at that moment that the moon chose to come out, and I saw that we were bending over the corpse of a man, who, by his dress and his presence in the courtyard, I took to be a servant of Francoise de Bretagny.

"Does he live?" I asked.

"Nay," replied John Stuart. "Strangled, by the look of his face and the marks on his throat—strange, those marks. There's something about them out of the ordinary. Have you flint and steel, lass?"

For answer, I drew flint and steel from the pouch at my waist and struck sharply. Briefly a spark flared, bathing the bloted face of the corpse in pale yellow light. Briefly, but long enough to show us what we saw. I gasped at the sight of the marks on the dead man's throat.

"By all that the Saints hold sacred," John Stuart said. "'Tis an enemy we're against that I would rather not be facing, Dark Agnes. For such is my thought. Mayhap ye'd best go back and find your way out of this cursed town—"

"What was it you saw, John Stuart?"

"Have you not eyes of your own, lass?"

"I saw—but I would hear it from your lips."

"Then hear it. I saw the marks of a hand against the throat of this corpse, and the marks of that hand were missing a finger."

"The hand of the dead sorcerer Costranno?" I said. "But how could that be? We saw him dead, the marks of the rope as plain upon his neck as the marks of the hand upon this poor man's neck."

"That jewel—" John Stuart said. "Saint Andrew! A magician is out to avenge Costranno, but it is not a friend of his but Costranno himself. Necromancy is the only answer. That alleyway where you were attacked. I have heard that the stones paving that alley were taken from an ancient heathen tample that once stood in a grove outside the city.

"It leaves me cold to think on it, but if but a tenth the tales related about Costranno be true, then he's magician enough to accomplish this and more. Mayhap his friends were not bearing him to his own house, but to that alley with its heathen temple's stones. Aye, mayhap they cut him from the gallows and were bringing him there. Likely Pelligny had even spoke the incantation to bring the dead to life when those footpads interrupted before he could place the jewel—the last step in the ritual. And that was accomplished when the jewel fell from your fingers on to the breast of the corpse."

"The holy saints!" I cried. "Then, I am a part of this. But even so, I swear that jewel slipped not from my fingers, but was yanked by *something,* some power!"

"By something from beyond the grave," Stuart said grimly, as he rose. "Now you go back and find your way to the waterfront and flee this city, for the watch will want your throat for a gibbet noose if you remain in Chartres."

"I cannot flee, for whatever snatched that jewel from my hands has made me an accomplice to necromancy and blasphemy," I said, resenting also the implication that I should flee from danger while John Stuart stayed to face it. "Two against one will not be too great odds when the one is a magician returned from the grave."

John Stuart paused, and I half expected argument. But instead he said, "There's little time then. Costranno, once back from the dead, must have stripped the clothes from the thieve's corpse and set out straightway to find Francoise de Bretagny. We are lucky he chose the tavern we were in to ask directions, though he must have known this house from the stories I have heard."

"But not the quarter of the city he was in," I said. "It was a quarter populous with thieves and cutthroats, but they had no truck with Costranno, nor he with them. Let us hurry. Even now we may be too late!"

We found the door to the house open like the courtyard gate. I found candles and lit one. We were in a large parlor, splendidly furnished in a way that bespoke a householder of great wealth. But there was not time to note the splendor of the room and its hangings.

"This way," John Stuart said. He headed for the stairs and I followed after him.

We reached the top of the stairs, where the candle cast flickering red light among the black shadows of a narrow hallway. For but a second John Stuart paused, then pointed and said, "That door!"

At the end of the hall there was an open door. He rushed toward it and I followed after him, almost causing the candle to flicker out in my haste.

The room beyond the open door was a bedchamber, a lady's bedchamber, fully as lavish in its appointments as the parlor below. The bed was empty and the covers thrown onto the floor. Furniture was overturned and a mirror broken, as if some thrown object had struck it instead of the target it was meant for. There was no sign of Francoise de Bretagny, nor of Costranno.

"What sorcery is this? Has he vanished into the air and taken her with him?" I said. "They couldn't have gotten past us."

A noise came from the darkness at my side, so sudden and unexpected that I almost dropped the candle as I whirled to face the source of the sound. I held the candle high to bathe a dark corner with light, and there in the corner was a man, cowering and gibbering, as a frightened child might gibber.

The man drew back against the wall as John Stuart approached him. The servant uttered sounds but they were meaningless sounds, such as are not pleasant to hear from the lips of a living man. I felt a shudder pass involuntarily up my spine and saw that even John Stuart was slightly unnerved by this, for as he turned back to face me the light from the candle was sufficient to show the strain upon his face.

"His mind is gone," Stuart said. He stood for a moment, those piercing eyes of his sweeping the room in a way that almost convinced me those shadows could conceal naught from him. "Aye," he said suddenly. "It's all so plain to me now. Obviously Francoise de Bretagny saw the need for protection, because both the servants we have seen were dressed and obviously set to guard her through the night. But the magnitude of the danger that beset her she did not begin to guess, else she would have fled the city—and indeed all of France. For now one of her servant-guards lies dead and the other's mind has fled him at the sight of a dead man carrying off his mistress. And she has been taken—but who can say where?"

"More than likely," I said, "it is too late now to save Francoise de Bretagny though we can avenge her murder."

"There may be time," John Stuart said, "if we make haste!" He began moving around the room, peering here and there, tapping the walls, feeling along the woodwork and behind hangings. "My guess is that Costranno has more sinister plans for her than murder, else her corpse would be sprawled across that bed. It may even be that some further ritual is necessary to fully revive him from the dead and that he has marked Francoise de Bretagny for that foul ceremony. Ah! What is this?"

His hand had reached behind a torn hanging and I could see that he moved something, though what it was he moved was hidden to me by the hanging. But as he moved it, a part of the wall moved out, revealing a passageway and beyond the passageway, a stair, leading down.

"This is how our necromancer made his escape," John Stuart said. From near the door, the maddened servant increased his gibbering, more frightened now than before. "Aye!" said John Stuart. "Our friend knows about this opening."

He stepped through the opening and I followed after him, holding high the candle to cast its light before us. "It is likely Francoise de Bretagny knew naught of this passageway," John Stuart said. "It may be that the entire city of Chartres is combed with passageways known only to Costranno and a few others."

"That is not a cheering thought," I said. "But I've a feeling there is more to it than I care for there to be."

The stairs were stone, seemingly carved from solid rock, leading down far below the level of the street, far deeper I felt than any cellar or dungeon in the city would be expected to go. The stairs wound down into the earth until I thought they would lead to hell itself, and then, ahead and below, we saw a light coming through a doorway at the foot of the stairs.

We paused momentarily upon the stairs and I strained my ears against the silence. For a moment it seemed deathly still, but then I thought a sound did come to me—the sound of a voice, perhaps, but too faint and muffled by distance and thick stone walls for me to be certain it was not the growling of some beast.

I snuffed out the candle I held and laid it carefully on the stairs. I was certain that the thickness of the walls around us would hide the sound of a candle dropping from any human ears, but I was not so certain that the ears the sound should be hidden from were human.

I drew my sword and followed John Stuart down the stairs.

We reached the bottom of the stairs and beyond the open door we saw a crypt, brightly lighted by torches set into brackets in the wall. I call it a crypt because there were caskets, or what appeared to be caskets, set into niches in the wall. But the writings and designs carved on these caskets and on the wall were not Christian, nor of any religion with which I am familiar. In the center of the crypt there was a dais of black marble and on the dais, naked and unconscious, but still breathing, lay Francoise de Bretagny. And a few feet away from the dais, Costranno himself knelt, straining to lift a seven sided stone in the floor. As we rushed through the doorway he saw us and gave one fierce inhuman effort that dragged the stone out of the floor and to one side, revealing a black, gaping hole.

Costranno's cloak was thrown off now, and his features, hidden to us in the tavern, were now revealed in the torchlight. The gibbet had done its work well. Bloated was the face of Costranno, his lips blacked with death had the marks and bite of the rope heavy upon his neck. He gave a great, incoherent cry as John Stuart moved toward him. Then the sorcerer fell back to the wall behind him and snatched a torch from its bracket. His unearthly, garbled voice rose in a shout that might have been rage or a call to the blasphemous gods he worshipped, and he threw the torch at Stuart.

The torch struck the brown stone flooring before John Stuart's feet with a shower of sparks and flames and a sudden billowing of black smoke. Instantly Stuart's figure was hidden from my view, but I could hear his voice, giving vent to his rage in a string of curses. The smoke was gone almost as suddenly as it came and Stuart still stood, apparently unhurt. But when he moved to leap at Costranno, something seemed to hold him back, as if an invisible wall had formed.

I spent no time in trying to fathom Costranno's magic. Before the sorcerer could reach another torch, I was upon him. And as Stuart cursed and raved because he could not move to hurl himself and his sword point upon his foe, I passed my sword twice through the undead man's body without harming him.

A horrible, angry cry came forth from Costranno's mangled throat. He drew his sword, and only my mail shirt beneath my doublet saved me from his terrible thrusts. But even so I was forced back, and the growling, snarling Costranno bore toward me, his sword slashing and beating at me with such terrific blows that I was hard put to parry.

I knew fear at that moment—icy, nerve-shattering fear that seemed to grip my very soul, and rendered me so senseless that I fought by instinct and main strength and without science or technique, save that of the moment. Costranno was in a rage and wanted my life and the life of John Stuart and of the naked, helpless girl who lay as intended sacrifice upon the black altar.

I did not realize his strategy until the heel of my left foot reached the edge of the opening in the floor behind me. Costranno had forced my back, hoping not to best me with the sword, but to hurtle me into the abyss. I knew nothing of what might be at the bottom of that pit, but somehow I knew that the kindest death that could befall one who toppled into it would be to have his body dashed to pieces at its bottom. I felt, but whatever power I cannot say, that there was something in that pit which I did not care to meet—and my fear became blind, unreasoning panic. And that is what saved me.

I hacked fiercely at Costranno, counting more on strength than skill, and in that moment drove him back far enough to give me the room I needed. I dove to one side, rolled and came to my feet behind him. I struck with all my strength, and the edge of my blade cut deep into the flesh of Costranno's mangled neck, severing through bone and gristle as well as flesh, and then pulling free as the severed head flopped from the shoulder of the corpse—and into the gaping blackness of the hole into which he had tried to push me.

There was an unearthly cry of terror from the blackness beneath the feet of the still standing corpse. Costranno's headless body stood for a moment at the edge of the pit and then on foot moved back, away from the edge.

My fear had become so agonizing that I was almost mindless, but somehow I saw what must be done and somehow brought myself to do it, despite the revulsion the thought of touching Costranno brought to me. I have fought many times and killed many men and seen many comrades die in battle. I have carried many a corpse to a shallow battlefield grave with no compunction about touching cold flesh. But the thought of touching a walking dead man was abhorrent in the extreme to me.

But it was necessary that I touch it so that it could not touch me. I forced myself to run up behind the shambling corpse and shove my hands hard against its shoulders. Something like a blast of lightning coursed through my body and threw me back, numbly, to the floor. But even as I fell to the floor, I saw the headless corpse topple into the pit.

For a moment there was silence in the chamber and neither Stuart or I moved. Then, on the altar, Francoise de Bretagny stirred and made a small, whimpering sound as consciousness started to return to her. John Stuart, free now of the spell which had imprisoned him, rushed to my side and reached down to aid me to my feet.

Suddenly shame at the womanly fear I had felt while fighting Costranno flooded me. Flustered, I shook off his hand and rose to my feet, unsteadily, but without help. "I'm all right," I said. "I can take care of myself."

John Stuart laughed, but there was, oddly nothing of contempt or malice in his laugh. "You are more a woman than you'll admit," he said. "And to your credit, Agnes de La Fere."

"If you would aid a helpless woman," I said, with discomfort, "then see to Francoise de Bretagny. My guess is we will need such influence as she can give us to gain protection from the watch before we escape this city."

"Aye," John Stuart said. "There is truth in what you say," He went to see to Francoise, and I stood, trying to conceal my nervousness, staring at the open pit in the floor.

I went to the wall and took a torch from a bracket and went to the edge of the opening and knelt down. I held the torch out over the opening and peered down into the blackness.

Before I knew what was happening, a snaky, black fur-covered arm reached out and grasped my doublet. I screamed as the arm strove to drag me into the hole and I beat down with the torch. There was a bestial cry and the thing let go. I had only a glimpse of a distorted, apish thing falling and the torch fell after, dwindling to a speck of light far below, like a meteor. I whimpered like a child and turned away from the pit into the welcome arms of John Stuart that closed about me like the protecting arms of some saint. And without shame I shivered for a time in those arms as my fear took hold of me and ran its course.

"It's over now, Dark Agnes," I heard the soothing deep voice of John Stuart. "And now you have naught to fear—and naught to be ashamed of. You have done as well against this horror as any woman or any man could do. And if, in the end, it comes to this, there is no shame for you to act as a woman, Dark Agnes, for you are quite a woman, indeed."

I did not object as he lifted me to my feet. "And it may chance," he went on, his voice now lighter and with that familiar hint of laughter to it, "that when you ride forth from this city, you will find me riding at your side."

"Do not forget the curse that hangs over me, John Stuart. Does it not bother you that the men who ride with Dark Agnes ride to an early grave?"

"Not a bit," John Stuart said, with booming laughter. "For what is another curse, more or less, upon the head of a Stuart!"

And together we replaced the stone slab in the opening in the floor and then helped Francoise de Bretagny from the crypt and up the stairs back to her own bedchamber, leaving behind the horror that pursued her.

THE KING'S SERVICE

THE SLOW rise and headlong fall of Rome shook the Western world. In the mushroom growth of the East, the downfall of imperial cities caused only a momentary ripple in the swarming tides of restless humanity, and their very memory faded from the minds of men even as the crawling jungle, the drifting desert, effaced the crumbling walls and shattered towers.

Such a kingdom, Nagdragore, whose eagle-crested rajahs levied tribute from the Deccan when yellow-haired barbarians were stalking red-handed through the gates of Rome.

The glories of Nagdragore have been forgotten for a thousand years. Not even in the misty gulf of the Hindu legend where an hundred lost dynasties sleep unheeded, does any hint of that vanished realm linger. Nagdragore is one with a thousand nameless ruins; a crumbling mass of shattered stone and broken marble, lost in the waving green deeps of the blind crawling jungle.

This tale is of the times of Nagdragore's lost splendor, before she decayed and fell before the ravages of White Hun, Tatar and Mogul; a tale of the Age that saw her gleam like a scintillant jewel on the dusky breast of India, when her imperial towers rose golden, white and purple in the blue, gazing with the pride of assured destiny across the green-girdling, white-foaming Gulf of Cambay.

* * * *

"The mists are clearing."

Hairy, calloused hands rested on long ash oars and frosty eyes peered through the thinning veil. The ship was a strange one for Eastern waters; it was long, lean, low in the waist, high of stern and bows, the prow curving up into a carved dragon's head. The open build, the shield-rail, the prow marked her as a raider as clearly as did her crew: huge, flaxen-bearded warriors with cold, light eyes.

On the poop stood a small group of men, and one of these, a brooding-eyed, lowering-browed giant, cursed in his beard.

"The hordes of Halheim know where we be, or in which direction be land; yet water and food grow scant—Hrothgar, you say you sense land to the eastward, but by Thor—"

A sudden shout went up from the crew, as the rowers set their oars aback and stared with dropped jaws. Before them the fog was thinning swiftly and now hanging in the dim sky a sudden blaze of gems and marble burst upon their eyes. They glimpsed, awedly, the turrets and spires and battlements of a mighty city in the sky.

"By the blood of Loki!" swore the Viking chief, "It's Mdigaard!"

Another on the poop laughed. The Viking turned to him irritably. This man was unlike his companions; he alone bore no weapons and wore no mail, yet the rest eyed him with a sort of sullen respect. There was in his bearing a natural, lion-like dignity, a nobility of manner and a realization of power without arrogance. He was tall, as broad-shouldered and powerful as any man there, and there was about him a certain cat-like litheness that most of the massive-limbed warriors lacked. His hair was golden as theirs, his eyes as blue, but no one would have mistaken him for one of them. His strong face, browned by the sun, was quick and mobile with the whimsical half-mockery of the Celt.

"Donn Othna," said the pirate chieftain angrily, "What is your jest now?"

The other shook his head. "I only laughed to think that in yon blaze of beauty a Saxon could see the city of his cold, savage gods who build with swords and skulls rather than marble and gold."

The breeze lifted the mists and the city shone more clearly. Port, harbor and walls grew out of the fading grey with astonishing swiftness.

"Like a city of a dream," muttered Hrothgar, his cold eyes strange with wonder. "The fog was thicker than we thought, that we should have so nearly approached such a port unknowing. Look at the craft which throng her wharves. What now, Athelred?"

The giant scowled. "They have already spied us; if we flee now we will have a score of galleys swooping after us, I think. And we must have fresh water—what think you, Donn Othna?"

The Celt shrugged his mighty shoulders.

"Who am I to think anything? I am no chief among you—but if we cannot flee—and to turn now would in sooth arouse suspicion—we must put on a bold front. I see yonder many trading crafts which have the look of far-farers and it may be that these people trade with many nations and will not fall on us at sight. Not all folk are Saxons!"

Athelred snarled churlishly and shouted at the steersman who had been resting on the long sweep, staring a-gape. The long ash oars began to churn the waves again and the galley boldly swept toward the dreaming harbor. Already other crafts were putting out to meet them. Strangely-built, richly-carved galleys manned by dark-skinned men swept upon alongside and the Saxons perforce lay to, while Athelred hailed their leaders.

The Vikings gazed in amazement at the costly-ornamented ships, and at the hawk-faced, turbaned warriors whose apparel shone in silver and silk, and whose weapons shimmered with gold chasings and sparkling gems; they gaped at the heavy steel bows, the round silver-spiked, gold-braced bucklers, the long slim spears, and curved sabers. And meanwhile the Orientals stared back in equal wonder at these white-skinned, flaxen-haired giants, with their horned helmets, scale mail shirts and flaring-edged axes.

A tall, black-bearded chief stood on the ornate deck of the nearer craft and shouted to Athelred who answered him in his own tongue. Neither could understand the other and the Saxon chief began to fume with the dangerous impatience of the barbarian. There was tension in the air. The Vikings stealthily laid down their oars and felt for their axes, and aboard the other crafts bowstrings slid into the nocks of barbed arrows. Then Donn Othna, on a long chance, shouted a greeting in the

Latin tongue. A change was instantly seen in the opposing chief.

He waved his arm and answered with a single word in the same tongue, which Donn Othna took to mean a friendly reply. The Celt spoke further, but the chief repeated the single Latin word and with a wave of his arm, indicated that the strangers should precede him into the port. The carles, at a growl from their chief, again took up their oars and the dragon-ship swept into the harbor and alongside the wharf with an escort of wallowing galleys on either side.

There the Eastern chief came alongside and by gesture indicated that they were to stay aboard their own craft for a while. Athelred's beard bristled at this, but there was nothing else to do. The chief strode away with a clatter of weapons and a number of tall, bearded warriors unobstrusedly 'took up their position on the wharves. They appeared not to notice the strangers, but Donn Othna noted that they outnumbered the dragon-ship's crew and that they bore wicked bows.

A great concourse of people came upon the wharves, gesticulating and shouting in wonder, gazing wide-eyed at the grim white giants who stared back equally fascinated. The archers thrust back the crowd roughly, forcing them to leave a wide space clear. Donn Othna smiled; more than his more stolid companions did he appreciate the gaudy panorama of color before him.

"Donn Othna," it was Athelred growling beside him, "on which side stand you?"

"What do you mean?"

The giant waved a huge hand toward the warriors on the wharves.

"If it comes to a pitched battle, will you fight for us or will you stab me in the back?"

The big Celt laughed cynically. "Strange words to a

prisoner. What avail would be a single sword against you hosts?" Then his manner changed. "Bring me the sword your men took from me; if I am to aid you I would not seem a thrall in the eyes of these people."

Athelred growled in his beard at the abrupt command, but his eyes fell before the cold gaze of the other and he shouted a command. A huge warrior presently mounted the poop, bringing with him a long heavy sword in a leather sheath, attached to a broad silver-buckled belt. Donn Othna's eyes sparkled as he took the weapon and fastened it about his waist. He laid hand on the jeweled ivory hilt with its heavy silver cross-guard and drew it half from the scabbard. The double-edged blade, of a sinister blue, hummed faintly.

"By Thor!" muttered Hrothgar. "Your sword sings, Donn Othna!"

"It sings for its homecoming, Hrothgar," answered the Celt. "Now I know that yon shore is the land of Hind, for it was here that my sword was born from furnace and forge and wizard's hammer, dim ages ago. It was once a great saber belonging to a mighty Eastern emperor, whom Alexander conquered. And Alexander took it with him into Egypt where it abode until the Romans came and a consul took it for his own. Not liking the curved shape, he had a sword-maker of Damascus reshape the blade—for the Romans used straight thrusting swords. It came into Britain with Caesar and was lost to the Gaels in a great battle in the west. I myself took it from Eochaidh Mac Ailbe, king of Erin, whom I slew in a sea-fight off the western coast."

"A sword for a prince," said Hrothgar in open admiration. "Look—one comes!"

With a great shouting and clanking of arms, a mighty concourse swept down to the wharves. A thousand warriors in shining armor, on Arab barbs, camels and grunting elephants escorted one who sat in a throne-like chair high on the back of a great elephant. Donn Othna saw a lean, haughty face, black-bearded and hawk-nosed; deep dark eyes, liquid and yet keen surveyed the westerners. The Celt realized that this king, lord or whoever he was, was not of the same race as his subjects.

The cavalcade halted before the dragon-ship, trumpets split the skies in a ripping fanfare, cymbals clashed deafeningly and then a gaudily dressed chieftain spurred forward, salaamed deeply from his saddle and burst into a grandiloquent flight of words which meant exactly nothing to the gaping Occidentals. The personage on the throne-chair checked his vassal with a languid wave of a white, jewel-decked hand and spoke in clear, liquid Latin:

"He is saying, my friends, that the exalted son of the gods, the great rajah Constantius, does you the stupendous, unheard of and entirely astounding honor of coming to greet you in person."

All eyes turned toward Donn Othna, the only man aboard the long-serpent who could understand the words. The huge Saxons eyed him eagerly like great, puzzled children and it was on him that the eyes of the Orientals focussed. The tall Celt stood, arms folded, head thrown back, meeting the gaze of the rajah squarely, and for all the splendor and trappings of the Oriental, his kingship was no less apparent than the royalty of the westerner. There two natural born leaders of men faced each other, recognizing each other's regal birthright.

"I am Donn Orthna, a prince of Britain," said the Celt. "This chief is Athelred of the Saxons. We have sailed for many a weary moon and desire only peace and a chance to trade for food and water. What city is this?"

"This is Nagdragore, one of the chief principalities of India," answered the rajah. "Come ashore; ye are my guests. It's many a day since I turned my face eastward

and I am hungry to speak with one in the old tongue of
Rome and hear the news of the west."

"What says he? Is it peace or war? Where be we?" the
questions rained on the Briton.

"We are indeed in the land of Hind," answered Donn
Othna. "But yonder king is not Indian. If he be a Greek,
then I am a Saxon! He bids us be his guests ashore; that
may well mean prisoners, but we have no choice. Mayhap
he means to deal fairly with us."

1

DONN OTHNA lifted a cup carved of a single jewel and drank deeply. He set it down and gazed across the richly carved teakwood table at the rajah who lounged sensuously on the silken divan. They were alone in the room except for the huge black mute who, naked except for a silk loincloth, stood just behind Constantius, holding a wide-bladed scimitar nearly as long as himself.

"Well, prince," said the rajah, toying idly with a great sapphire on his finger, "have I not played squarely with you and your men? Even now they gorge and guzzle on such meat and drink as they never dreamed existed, and rest themselves on silken couches, while musicians play stringed music for their pleasure and girls lithe as panthers dance for them. I have not even taken their axes from them—as for you, here you feast with me alone—yet I see suspicion in your eyes."

Donn Othna indicated the sword which he had unbuckled and laid on a polished bench.

"I had not unslung Alexander's sword did I not trust you. As for the Saxons—Crom's jest! They are like bears in a palace. Had you sought to disarm them their wonder had turned to desperate rage and those same axes had drunk deep in the red tides. It is not suspicion you see in my eyes but wonder. By the gods! When I was a shock-headed boy on the western marches I wondered at Tara in Erin, and gaped at Caer Odun. Then when I was a youth and raided into Roman territory, I thought Corinium, Aquae Sulis, Ebbracum and Lundinium were the mightiest cities of all the earth. When I came into manhood the memory of those was paled by my first sight of Rome, though it was crumbling under the defiling feet of Goth and Vandal. And Rome seems but a village when I gaze at the crowned spires and golden-chased towers of Nagdragore!"

Constantius nodded, a tinge of bitterness in his eyes. "It is an empire worth fighting for, and once I had dreams of spanning the land of India from sea to sea—but tell me of Rome and Byzantium; it has been a long time since I turned my face eastward. Then the German barbarians were overrunning the Roman borders, Genseric was pillaging the imperial city herself and rumors of a strange and terrible people came even to Byzantium which writhed under the heel of the Ostrogoth."

"The Huns!" exclaimed Donn Othna, his face lighting fiercely. "Aye, they came out of the East like a wind of death—like a swarm of locusts. They drove the Goths, the Franks and the Vandals before them and the Teutons trampled Rome in their flight. Then with the sea before them, they could fly no further. They turned at bay, the two hosts met at Chalons—by the gods, there was a sword-quenching! There the ravens fed and the axes were glutted redly! They rolled on us like a black wave, and as a wave breaks on the rocks, they broke on the German shield wall and the ranks of Aetius' legions."

"You were there?" exclaimed Constantius.

"Aye! With five hundred of my tribesmen!" Donn Othna's fierce eyes blazed and he smote his fist resoundingly upon the table. "We sailed with those British legions who went to the succor of Rome—and came no more to their native soil. On the plains of Gaul and Italy their bones rot—and those of many a western clansman who never bowed to Rome, but who followed his civilized kin to the wars.

"All day we fought and at the end, the Huns broke; by Crom, my sword was red and clotted from pommel to point, and I could scarcely lift my arm. Of my five hundred warriors, fifty lived!

"Well, Votigern had called in the Jutes to aid him against the Picts and the Angles, and Saxons followed them like hungry wolves. I returned to Britain and in the whirlwind of war that swept the southern coasts, I fell captive to this Athelred, who knowing my name and rank, wished to hold me for ransom. But a strange thing came to pass—"

Donn Othna paused and laughed shortly.

"We of the west hate long and well, and our Gaelic cousins make a cult of revenge, but by Crom, I never knew what the lust for vengeance could be until we sighted the ships of Asgrimm the Angle. This sea-king has an old feud with Athelred and he gave chase with his ten long-serpents. By Crom, he chased us half around the world! He hung to our stern like a hunting dog and we could not elude him.

"We raced him around the coast of Gaul and down past Spain, and when we would have turned into the Mediterranean he crowded us close and drove us past the

Gates of Hercules. South and forever south we fled, past sullen, steaming coasts, dank with swamp or dark with jungle, where black people wild and naked shouted and shot arrows at us.

"At last we rounded a cape and headed east, and somewhere there we shook off our pursuers. Since then we have sailed and rowed at random. So you see, King Constantius, my news is nearly a year old."

The rajah's deep dark eyes were pensive with inner thought. He sighed and drank deep of the goblet the black slave filled and tasted first.

"Nearly twenty years ago I sailed from Byzantium with Cyprian traders bound for Alexandria. I was but a youth, ignorant and full of wonder at the world, but with royal blood in my veins. From Alexandria I wandered by devious ways to Damascus and there I joined a caravan returning to Shiraz in Persia. Later I sought pearls on the Gulf of Oman and it was there that I was taken captive by a Maldive pirate who sold me on the slave block at Nagdragore. I need not repeat to you the devious route by which I reached the throne.

"The old dynasty was crumbling, ready to fall; Nagdragore was harried by incessant wars with neighboring kingdoms. It was a red trail, black with plot and treachery that I followed, but today I am rajah of Nagdragore—though the throne rocks beneath my feet."

Constantius rested his elbows on the table and his chin in his hands; his great brooding eyes fixed themselves on the blond giant opposite him.

"You are a prince likewise, though your palace be a wattle hut," he said. "We be of the same world, though I had my birth at one end, and you at the other end of that world. I need men I can trust. My kingdom is divided against itself and I play one chief against the other to the hurt of Nagdragore, but to mine own gain. My chief foes are Anand Mulhar and Nimbaydur Singh. The one is rich, cowardly and avaricious; too cautious and too suspicious to oppose me openly. The other is young, passionate, romantic and brave, but a victim of moneylenders who watch the way the fish leaps.

"The common people hate me because they love Nimbaydur Singh who has a trace of royal blood in his veins. The nobles—the Rajputs—dislike me because I am an outlander. But I rule the moneylenders, and through them, Nagdragore.

"The war is a more or less secret one in which I am ground between Anand Mulhar on the one side and Nimbaydur Singh on the other, yet still hold in my hands the reins of power. They hate each other too much to combine against me.

"But it is the silent assassin's dagger I have to fear. I half trust my guard, but half trust is little better than full suspicion and far more dangerous. That is why I came down to the wharves to greet you myself. Will you and these barbarians remain here in the palace and do battle for me if the occasion arise?

"I could not make you officially my bodyguard. It would offend the nobles and all would rise instantly. But I will ostensibly make you part of the army; you will remain here in the palace and you, prince, shall be my cup companion."

Donn Othna grinned a slow, lazy grin, and reached for the wine pitcher.

"I will talk to Athelred," said he. "I think he will agree."

2

THE BRITON found Athelred sitting cross-legged on a silken couch, tearing at a huge quarter of roast lamb, between enormous gulps of Indian wine. The Saxon growled a greeting and continued to gorge and guzzle, while Donn Othna seated himself and glanced quizzically about him. The pirate crew sprawled at ease among the cushions on the marble floor or wandered about the great room, gazing curiously up at the jeweled dome high overhead or staring out the golden-barred windows into courts with flowering trees and exotic blossoms scenting the air, or into colonnaded chambers where fountains flung a silvery sheen high into the air. They were curious and delighted as children and suspicious as wolves. Each kept his curved-handled, wicked-headed axe close to his hand.

"What now, Donn Othna?" mumbled Athelred, munching away without a pause.

"What would you?" parried the Briton.

"Why," the pirate waved a half-gnawed bone about him, "here's loot that would make Hengist's eyes open and Cerdic's mouth water. Let us do this: in the night we will rise stealthily and set fire to the palace; then in the confusion we will snatch such plunder as we can easily bear away and hack our way to our ship which lies unguarded along the docks. Then, ho, for the western seas! When my people see what we bring, there will be a hundred dragon-ships following us! We will plunder Nagdragore as Genseric plundered Rome and carve us out a kingdom with our axes."

"Would it draw your sea-wolves from Britain," said Donn Othna grimly, "I might agree. But it's a plan too mad for even a Saxon to try. Even if I could overlook the treachery to our host, we could never cover half the distance to the ship. A hundred and fifty men cut their way through fifty thousand? Think no more of it."

"What then?" growled Athelred. "By Thor, it seems our positions have changed! Aboard ship you were our prisoner. Now it seems we are yours! We are hereditary foes; how do I know you mean to deal squarely with us? How do I know what you and the king have been jabbering to each other? Maybe you plan to cut our throats."

"And not knowing you must take my word for it," answered the prince calmly. "I have no love for you or your race, though I know you as brave men. But here it is to our advantage to act in concert. Without me you have no interpreter; without you I have no armed force to strengthen my claim to respect. Constantius has offered us service in his palace guards. I trust him no more than you trust me; he will deal us false the moment it is to his advantage. But until such time it is to our advantage to comply with his request. If I know men, niggardliness is not one of his faults. We will live well on his bounty. Just now he needs our swords. Later that need may pass and we may take ship again—but understand, Athelred, this service I do you now is my ransom. I am no longer your prisoner and if I go aboard your ship again, I am a free man, whom you will set on British soil without price."

"I swear it by my sword," grunted Athelred, and Donn Othna nodded, satisfied, knowing the blunt Saxon was a man of his word.

"The East is fraught with unlimited possibilities," said the Briton. "Here a bold heart and a keen sword can accomplish as much as they can in the West and the reward is greater, if more fleeting. Just now, I doubt if Constantius trusts me fully. I must prove that we can be of value to him."

The chance came sooner than he had hoped. In the days following, Donn Othna and his comrades abode in the mazes of the Eastern city, wondering at the strange contrasts: the splendor and riches of the nobles, the poverty and squalor of the poor. Nor was the least paradox he who sat upon the throne.

Donn Othna sat in the golden-leaf chamber and drank wine with the rajah Constantius, while the great silent black man served them. The British prince gazed in wonder at the rajah. Constantius drank deeply and unwisely. He was drunk, his strange eyes darker and more liquid than ever.

"You are a relief as well as a protection to me, Donn Othna," said he, with a slight hiccup. "I can be my true self with you—at least I assume it to be my true self. I trust you because you bring the clean, straightforward power of the western winds and the clean salt tang of the western seas with you. I need not be forever on my guard. I tell you, Donn Othna, this business of empire is not one that makes for ease or happiness. Had I to live my life over again, I would rather be what once I was: a clean-limbed, brown-skinned youth, diving for pearls in the Oman Gulf and flinging them away to dark-eyed Arab girls.

"But the purple is my curse and my birthright, just as it's yours. I am rajah not because I was wise or foolish but because I have the blood of emperors in my veins and I followed a destiny I could not avoid. You, too, will live to press a throne and curse the crown that wearies your tired neck. Drink!"

Donn Othna waved away the proffered goblet.

"I have drunk enough and you far too much," he said bluntly. "By Crom, I have found to be much of a hashish eater and more of a drunkard. You are incredibly wise and incredibly foolish. How can a man like you be a king?"

Constantius laughed. "A question that had cost another man his head. I will tell you why I am king: because I can flatter men and see through their flattery; because I know the weaknesses of strong men; because I know how to use money; because I have no scruples whatever, and resort to any method, fair or foul, to gain my ends. Because, being born to the West and raised in the East, the guile of both worlds is in me. Because, though I am in the main a fool, I have flashes of real genius, beyond the power of a consistently wise man. And because—and all my other gifts were useless without it—I have the power of molding women as wax in my hands. Let me look in any woman's eyes and hold her close to me, and she is my slave forever."

Donn Othna shrugged his mighty shoulders and set down his goblet.

"The East draws me with a strange fascination," said he, "though I had rather rule a tribe of shock-headed Cymry. But, by Crom, your ways are devious and strange."

Constantius laughed and rose unsteadily. The retiring of the rajah was attended to only by the great black mute. Donn Othna slept in a chamber adjoining the golden-leaf room.

And now Donn Othna, dismissing his own slave, stepped to the heavily barred window that looked out on an inner court, and breathed deep the spice scents of the Orient. The dreaming antiquity of India touched his eyelids with slumberous fingers and in the deeps of his soul dim racial memories stirred. After all, he felt a certain kinship with these hawk-faced, keen-eyed Rajputs. They were of his blood, if the ancient legends were true that told of the days when the sons of Aryan were one great tribe in the mist-dim ages before Nimbaydur Singh's ancestors broke from the nation in that great southern drift, and before Donn Othna's ancestors took up the long trek westward.

A faint sound brought him back to the present. A quick stride took him across the room where he gazed into the golden-leaf chamber through a cloth-of-gold curtain. A dancing girl had entered the chamber and Donn Othna wondered how she had gotten past the swordsmen stationed outside the door. She was a slim young thing, lithe and beautiful, her scanty silken girdle and golden breastplates accentuating her sinuous loveliness. She approached the huge black who stared at her in sullen wonder and menace. She approached him, her red lips pleading, her deep eyes luring, her little hands outstretched and upturned beseechingly. Donn Othna could not understand her low tones—though he had learned much of the Rajput language—but he saw the black shake his bullet head and lift his huge scimitar threateningly.

She was close to the mute now—and she moved like a striking cobra. From somewhere about her scanty garments she flashed a dagger and with the same motion

she flicked it under the mute's heart. He swayed like a
great black idol, the sword fell from his nerveless hands
and he fell across it, his face writhing in the agony of effort
as his withered tongue sought to sound a warning to his
master. Then blood burst from that silently gaping mouth
and the great slave lay still.

The girl sprang quickly and silently toward the door,
but Donn Othna was ahead of her in a single bound. She
checked herself for a fleeting second, then sprang at his
throat like a fury. The dances of the East make their
devotees lithe and steel-like in every thew. Ages later
when westerners again invaded the East, they found that a
slim nautch girl could prove more than a match for a man.
But those men had never tugged at a galley oar, wielded a
twenty pound battle-axe or reined four wild chariot
horses back on their haunches. Donn Othna caught the
feline fury that was thrusting so earnestly for his life,
disarmed her with little effort and tucked her under his
arm like a child.

He was rather uncertain as to his next step when out of
the royal bedchamber came the rajah, his eyes still
clouded somewhat with wine. A single glance showed him
what had occurred.

"Another woman assassin?" he asked casually. "My
throne against your sword, Donn Othna, Anand Mulhar
sent her. Nimbaydur Singh is too upright for such
tricks—the poor fool." He casually touched the body of
his faithful slave with his toe, but made no comment.

"What shall I do with the spit-fire?" asked Donn
Othna. "She's too young to hang and if you let her go—"

Constantius shook his head. "Neither one nor the
other; let me have her."

Donn Othna handed her to the rajah as if she were an
infant, glad to be rid of the scratching, biting little devil.

But at the first touch of Constantius' hands she fell quiet, trembling like a high-strung steed. The rajah sat down on a divan and forced the girl to her knees before him, without harshness and without mercy. She whimpered a little, far more afraid of the Greek's calmness than she had been of Donn Othna's anger. One white jeweled hand held her slim wrist, the other rested on her head forcing her to look up into the rajah's face with eyes that sought desperately to escape his steady stare.

"You are very young and very foolish," said Constantius in a deliberate tone. "You came here to murder me because some evil master sent you—" his hand slowly caressed her as a man pets a dog. "Look into my eyes; I am your rightful master. I will not harm you; you will remain with me and you will love me."

"Yes, master," the girl answered in a small voice like a girl in a trance; her eyes did not try to evade Constantius now. They were very wide and filled with a strange new light; she leaned to the rajah's caress. He smiled and the quality of that smile made him strangely handsome.

"Tell me who you are and who sent you," he commanded, and to Donn Othna's utter amazement, the girl bowed her head obediently.

"I am Yatala; my master Anand Mulhar sent me to kill you, master. For more than a moon now, I have danced in the palace. For my master put me on the block and so contrived that your wizard bought me among other dancing girls. It was well planned, master. I came tonight and made eyes at the guards without; then when they let me approach, seeing that I was little and unarmed, I blew a secret dust into their eyes, so that deep sleep came upon them. Then taking a dagger from one, I entered—and you know the rest, master."

She hid her face on Constantius' knees and the rajah

looked up at Donn Othna with a lazy smile.

"What think you of my power over women now, Donn Othna?"

"You are a devil," answered the prince frankly. "I would have taken oath no torture could have wrung from that girl what she has just told you freely—hark!"

A stealthy footstep sounded without. The girl's eyes flared with sudden terror.

"Beware, my lord!" she cried. "That is Tamur, Anand Mulhar's strangler; he followed me to make sure—"

Donn Othna whirled toward the door—it opened to reveal a terrible shape. Tamur was taller and heavier than the powerful Briton. Naked except for a loincloth, his dusky bronze skin rippled over knots and coils of iron muscles. His limbs were like oak and iron, yet lithe and springy as a tiger's, his shoulders incredibly wide. A short tree-like neck held a bestial head. The low, slanting forehead, the flaring nostrils, the cruel gash of a mouth, the close-ears, the ape-like shaven skull, all betrayed the human beast, the born bloodletter. In his girdle was twisted the implement of his trade: a sinister silken cord. In his right hand he bore a curved saber.

Donn Othna took in this formidable figure in one glance, then he was springing to the attack with the headlong savagery of his race. His sword flashed through the air in a blazing blue arc just as the other struck. Here was no hesitant caution on either side. Both sprang and struck simultaneously, quick to fling all on a single blow. And in mid-air the curved blade and the straight blade met with a resounding clash. The scimitar shivered to a thousand ringing sparks and, before the Briton could strike again, the strangler dropped his hilt and like a striking snake caught his white-skinned foe in a fierce grip.

The British prince let go his sword, useless at such close

quarters, and returned the grapple. In an instant he knew that he was pitted against a skilled and cruel wrestler. The smooth, naked body of the Indian was like a great snake and as hard to hold. But not for naught had Donn Othna held his own with trained Roman wrestlers of old. Now he blocked and fended shrewd thrust of knee and elbow and the clutch of iron fingers that sought cruel, maiming holds, while he launched an attack of his own. The thin veneer of civilization, acquired from contact with his Romanized neighbors, had vanished in the heat of battle, and it was a white-skinned barbarian, wild as any Goth or Saxon, who tore and snarled in the golden-leaf room of Nagdragore's rajahs.

Donn Othna saw, over Tamur's heaving shoulder, Constantius approaching with the sword he had dropped and, blue eyes blazing with battle-lust, he snarled for the rajah to keep back and let him finish his own fight.

Chest to chest, the giants strove, reeling back and forth, close-clinched, but still upright, each foiling every effort of the other. Tamur's thumb gouged at Donn Othna's eye, but the prince sank his head against the other's massive chest, shifted his hold, and the strangler was forced to cease gouging and break the Briton's hold, to save his own spine.

Again Tamur caught Donn Othna's arm in a sudden bone-breaking crossbar grip that had snapped the elbow like a twig had not the British prince suddenly driven his head hard and desperately into the Indian's face. Blood spattered as Tamur's head snapped back and Donn Othna, following his advantage, back-heeled him and threw him. Both crashed heavily on the floor, but the strangler writhed from under the Briton, and the latter found his neck menaced by a grip that bent his head back at a sickening angle.

With a gasp he tore free, just as Tamur drove his knee

agonizingly into the Briton's groin. Then as the white man's iron grip involuntarily relaxed, the brown man leaped free, whipping the deadly cord from his girdle. Donn Othna rose more slowly, nauseated with the pain of that foul thrust, and Tamur, with an inhuman croak of triumph, sprang and cast his cord. The Briton heard the girl scream, as he felt the thin length whip like a serpent about his throat, instantly cutting off his breath. But at the same instant he struck out blindly and terrifically, his clenched iron fist meeting Tamur's jaw like a mallet meeting a ship's side. The strangler dropped like a log and Donn Othna, gasping, tore the cord from his tortured throat and flung it aside, just as Tamur scrambled to his feet, eyes glaring like a madman's.

The Briton fell on him raging, battering him with sledge-hammer blows, gained from long hours of practice with cestus. Such an attack was beyond Tamur's skill to cope with; the East has not the instinct of striking with the clenched fist. A swing that smashed full in his mouth splattered blood and splintered teeth and he retaliated with the only sort of blow he knew—an open-handed, full-armed slap to the side of the head that staggered Donn Othna and filled his eyes with momentary spark-short darkness. But instantly he returned the blow with a smash that sank deep in Tamur's midriff and dropped him to his knees, gasping and writhing.

The strangler grappled Donn Othna's legs and dragged him down, and once more they battled and tore close-clinched. But the ravening Briton felt his foe grow weaker and, redoubling the fury of his attack, like a tiger maddened by the blood scent, he bore the Indian backward and down, sought and found a deadly hold at last and strangled the strangler, sinking his iron fingers deeper and deeper until he felt the life flow out from under them and the writhing body stiffened.

Then Donn Othna rose and shook the blood and sweat from his eyes and smiled grimly at the spellbound rajah who stood like one frozen, still dangling Alexander's sword.

"Well, Constantius," said Donn Othna, "you see I am worthy of your trust."

THE SHADOW OF THE HUN

Prologue

A CALM held the great warship in a level ring of the landless sea. The brass and gold work glittered in the sun, the idle sails flapped against the mast. On the high-flung poop three men sipped wine and conversed idly. Save for one feature, they were types as far apart as might be imagined, but in one way they were alike: each had the appearance of the born warrior.

Athelstane the Saxon was a giant; six and a half feet he towered from his sandals of bull's hide to his shock of flaxen hair. His crisp beard was as golden as the massive armlets he wore, his eyes large, calm and grey. He wore a corselet of scale mail and even as he drank and talked, he held across his knees his two-handed broadsword in its worn sheath.

Don Roderigo del Cortez was tall, dark and spare, clad in plain, unornamented armor. His dark eyes were deep and somber, his manner stately and courteous. He wore no beard but a thin mustache, and his only arm was a long narrow sword—forerunner of the rapier.

Turlogh Dubh O'Brien was not as tall as either of his companions, though he was well over six feet. His dark face was clean shaven, his black hair cropped short. From under heavy black brows gleamed his volcanic eyes—blue, and full of shifting gleams like clouds passing across some deep blue lake. Long-limbed, deep-chested, broad-shouldered, his every motion betokened his iron strength and cat-like litheness. He was, in some ways, more the complete fighting man than his friends, for he possessed a dynamic quickness the Saxon lacked, and sheer strength beyond the power of the slender Spaniard.

He was armed in black, closely-worked chain mail, and a green girdle held a long dirk at his hip. Close by in a weapon rack rested more of his arms: a plain vizorless helmet with a mail drop, a round buckler with a keen spike in the center, and a single-handed axe. This axe partook of the lethal quality of its owner; with its keen single edge, perfectly made handle of oak that would notch a sword, it was the weapon of a master. It was lighter than most of the axes of the age, and built on different lines. A short keen spike on the back and one on the top of the head added to its deadly appearance.

"Don Roderigo," rumbled Athelstane, refilling his goblet, "what of these Easterners we are sailing against? Thor's blood, I have crossed steel with all the war-men of the Western world, but these I have not seen. Many of my comrades have fared to Mikligaard, but not I."

"The Saracens are brave and cruel warriors, good sir," answered the Don. "They fight with javelins and curved sabers. And they hate our fair Lord Christ, for they hold to Muhammad."

"As I gather it," pursued Athelstane, "east, whither we

are sailing, lies the neck of water which divides Europe from Africa. The infidel Saracens hold both Africa and the greater part of Spain. And beyond lies, on one side of the Middle Sea, Italy and Greece, and on the other the eastern part of Africa and Holy Land which the Arab jackals defile. And thereabouts is Constantinople, or Mikligaard as the Vikings name it—and beyond, what?"

Don Roderigo shook his head. "Beyond lies Iran— Persia—and the wilderness wherein swarm pagan Turks and Tatars. Beyond—they tell wild tales of Hind and Cathay—but who knows? Between lies deserts and mountains full of pagans and evil spirits, dragons and—"

Turlogh suddenly interrupted with a shake of his head. "There are no dragons, Don Roderigo, though truth to tell there are many perils for the wanderer, both from beast and men."

The others glanced curiously at him. It was not often the Gaelic outcast opened his lips to speak of his long wanderings. But now it was his mood.

"I was some seven years younger," said he, "when I sailed one day from Erin on a raid—by my axe, it was a lengthy raid, for it was more than three years ere I set foot again on Irish land. Mind you, Athelstane, in those days of my outlawry I had a ship of my own; aye, and a crew."

"I remember," muttered the Saxon. "My Viking comrades had scathe thereby and villages smoked on England's western coast. But what of the unknown lands to the east whereof I spoke?"

"If you land on the southeasternmost coast of the Baltic Sea," answered Turlogh O'Brien, "and wander southward and eastward, you will come to a great inland sea—the Caspian Sea. Between them lie a vast land of forest and rivers, and wide, rolling plains, with few trees but grown with tall grass—a vast, grey, desolate land—"

Across the leaden, grey steppes, beneath the grey,

leaden sky flew a few herons. As far as eye could reach stretched the drab, waving grass, ruffled by a chill wind. A few scanty clusters of stunted trees broke the monotony and in the distance there was discernible the outline of a great river that wound, serpent-like, through the wilderness. Reeds grew tall and thick there and waterfowl circled above.

Turlogh O'Brien gazed out across the wastes and the gloomy desolation entered into his soul. Then he started. Out of the growth about the river broke four figures, which his keen eyes made out as hosemen, racing toward him—one in advance of the others. Turlogh held in his hand the reins of a great roan stallion. Now he mounted swiftly, unslung axe and buckler and rode into a sparse clump of trees which stood nearby. He did not believe the oncoming riders were coming to attack him; their attitude was such as to make him believe that the three behind pursued the fourth. And the Gael was curious to know what manner of men inhabited this wilderness.

They approached swiftly and soon Turlogh saw that his surmise was correct. The man in front swayed in his saddle, and one arm dangled limply. He guided his steed with the other hand and held a broken sword between his teeth. He was tall and young and he rode like the wind, his shock of yellow hair flying in the breeze. But the pursuers were swiftly closing the gap. They were shorter in stature than he they hunted, and mounted on smaller, nimbler steeds. As they approached the Celt's refuge, Turlogh saw they were very dark, were clad in light silvered mail shirts and wore turbans. They bore light round shields and curved scimitars.

Turlogh's mind was made up in an instant. This was none of his quarrel; but yonder three armed men hunted a wounded warrior, who was certainly of a tribe more akin to Turlogh's own people, than the pursuers. These were

Turks, the Gael decided, though he had supposed their ranges to lie considerably more to the south. An instinctive hatred burned up in his breast. It was the old, old feud between Aryan and Turanian, so strong that it sends the distant descendants of primitive warriors at each others' throats.

Now the yellow-haired youth thundered past the scanty grove, and now the foremost of the pursuers was almost abreast it. A lifted scimitar gleamed in a dark hand and a fierce yell of triumph rose to the skies—to be changed to a gasp of surprise as an unexpected shape shot from the trees.

Like a bolt from a catapult, the great roan crashed full against the steed of the Turk. There was no time to rein about and avoid the impact. Striking from the side, the heavier horse hurled the lighter off its feet and headlong, flinging the rider underfoot where a lashing hoof dashed out his brains.

Turlogh reined about to meet the onset of the remaining Turks who howled like wolves in amazement and rage, but assailed him from either side. The Gael spurred to meet the nearest, ere the other could come at him from the other side. The curved scimitar lashed at Turlogh's head, but the Gael, guiding his horse with his knees, caught the blade on his shield and struck almost simultaneously. The keen edge bit through the turban and split the shaven skull beneath. As the Turk slumped from his saddle, Turlogh wheeled back to parry the scimitar that already hovered over him. The yellow-haired youth had seen the fray and was charging back to his rescuer's aid, but the fight was over before he could reach it.

The remaining Turk charged in from Turlogh's left, howling and hacking like a madman, believing the Gael could not reach him with his red axe without turning his steed or shifting the weapon to his left hand. But as he plunged in, slashing, the yellow-haired youth saw a trick of battle of which he had never heard. Turlogh rose in his stirrups, twisted in his saddle and reversed the usual procedure. He parried the whistling blade with his axe and struck with his buckler as a boxer strikes with a heavy cestus. The Turk's howl of triumph broke in a ghastly gurgle as the spike in the center of the shield tore his jugular vein. Blood flooded Turlogh's buckler and the Turk lurched to the earth where he died, clawing at his red-dabbled beard.

Turlogh turned to see the wounded youth reining his steed near. He spoke in a tongue the Gael could understand:

"I thank you, brother, whoever you are. These dog-brothers had carried my head back to Khogar Khan, had it not been for you. Four of them started me among the reeds of the river. One I slew—by Saint Piotr, he'll never eat sunflower seeds again. But they shattered my sword and broke my arm and I fled perforce. Tell me your name, that we may be brothers."

"My name is Turlogh Dubh, that is to say, Black Turlogh," answered the Gael. "My clan is the O'Brien, my land Erin. But now I am an outcast from my people and have wandered for many moons."

"I am Somakeld," said the youth, "and my people are the Turgaslavs, the steppes dwellers. My clan is camped just beyond yonder skyline. Come with me and let my people welcome you."

"Let me first see to that arm," said Turlogh, though the youth laughed at the scratch, as he called it. Turlogh, skilled in the dressing of wounds, set the broken bone and bandaged the deep saber slash as well as he could with mud and spiderwebs taken from the stunted trees. Somakeld uttered no murmur of complaint and when the task was done, thanked the Celt with quiet courtesy. Then they rode toward the Slavic camp.

"How is it you speak my tongue?" asked the lad.

"I have wandered for months among the great forests," answered Turlogh. "The forest tribes are akin to the steppes dwellers and their tongue is much the same. But tell me this, Somakeld, whence come those Turks we slew? I have seen Tatars, who ride even into the great forests sometimes, but I had thought that the empire of the Turks lies far to the south."

"Aye, so it does," agreed Somakeld. "But these dogs were driven out by their kin."

Somakeld spoke at some length, and Turlogh found him to be far more frank and keen witted than the sullen forest people his late wanderings had led him among. Though a youth, the young Slav had journeyed far "—to the yellow sands of the south, where the caravans ply behind Rhoum and Bokhara, east beyond the Blue Sea (the Aral Sea), beyond the northern reaches of the Volga, and west to the great river called the Dnieber." His was a wandering, nomadic tribe and he himself had more than his share of the wanderlust.

These Turks were wilder, fiercer cousins to the Seljuks before whose onslaught the Arab caliphates of Islam were crumbling. This particular tribe had been overthrown in the incessant border warfare, either by the Persians or by some kindred Turkish clan; Somakeld was not sure. But they had fled the pasture lands of their ancestors and had wandered far beyond the loose boundaries of their race.

They had come into the steppes where the nomadic outposts of two rival races bickered and mingled; where the easternmost drift of the last Aryan wanderers snarled and snapped at the westernmost drift of the Tatar herders. The usual desultory warfare had ensued: skirmishes and raids for women and horses on both sides. The roving bands of Tatars took first one side and then the other as their whims led them. But of late the war had taken on a new aspect. A new khan had arisen among the Turks who held the grazing lands beyond the river. This one was Khogar Khan, who gained his leadership by murdering the former khan. His ambition was great. He dreamed of power—of the sovereignty, not of a waste of grazing land and wandering tribes, but of a great empire, reaching from the heart of the steppes to the Caspian Sea. It was no mad vision, commented Somakeld, who had heard the old men talk of mushroom empires that sprang up almost overnight in the teeming mazes of the East, to sweep across the curve of the world like a prairie fire, and as quickly to burn itself out.

But Khogar Khan had one obstacle to overcome first: the Turgaslavs, hereditary lords of the steppes. His first, main step must be to crush them.

Already the Turks, fired by their warlike leader, had routed the Tatar clans in the vicinity, slaying many, forcing some into a sullen subjection and driving the rest away. Now the Moslems were gathering their forces for a powerful drive on their Aryan foes to the west. Riders were scouring the steppes, gathering the Turgaslavic clans. His people had no villages, Somakeld explained, but followed the grass. The various clans of the tribes were scattered wherever fancy might lead them, over a radius of a hundred miles.

Spies had reported the movements of the Turks, and it was while returning from a distant clan that Somakeld had encountered his hereditary foes. His tribe was not a large one, said the young Turgaslav, but for centuries they had overcome their foes. Once they numbered many thousands, but tribal wars had thinned them and branches of the tribe had split off and wandered westward, there to forget their pastoral life and become tillers of the soil. Somakeld sniffed in disdain.

"But you, my brother," he exclaimed suddenly, "you have not told me how you have come to wander alone so far from your own pasture land. Surely you were a chief among your own people." Turlogh grinned bleakly. "Once I was a chief in an island far to the west, called Erin. My king was an ancient man and very wise, and his name was Brian Boru. But the great king fell in a mighty battle with red-bearded sea-rovers called Danes, though his people won the battle. Then followed a time of feud and intrigue and the spite of a woman and the jealousy of a kinsman cast me forth from my clan, an outlaw to starve on the heath.

"But though I was no longer one of the Dal Cais, my heart was still bitter against the Danes who had ravaged my land for centuries and I drew to me certain masterless men and outlaws like myself, and by devious ways we took a galley from the Danes."

And with swift words Turlogh sought to picture for the young Slav that red phase in his restless and battle-haunted life.

His ship was *The Raven* which he re-named *Crom's Hate* after an old heathen Celtic god. Trickery and savage fighting won her, and the scum of the seas manned her. Not one of her crew but had a price on his head. To Turlogh flocked rogues and thieves and murderers, whose only virtue was the reckless abandon of desperate men who have nothing to live for.

Irish outlaws, Scottish criminals, runaway Saxon thralls, Welsh Freebooters, gallow's birds from Brittany—these steered and rowed *Crom's Hate* and fought and looted at their savage lord's command. There were men with cropped ears and slit noses, men with brands on face and shoulder, men whose limbs bore the marks of

rack and shackle. They were without love and without
hope and they fought like blood-hungry devils.

Their only law was the word of Turlogh O'Brien, and
that law was adamantine. There was no sentiment
between them; they snarled about him like wolves and he
cursed them for the vermin they were. But they feared and
respected his ferocity and fighting prowess and he
recognized their desperate savagery. He made no attempt
to impose his will upon them in ways of other leaders
whose hand is not against the world. He demanded of
them only that they follow him and fight like demons
when he gave the word. Nor did he give an order twice. In
the hellish environments in which he found himself, all the
slumbering tiger awoke in the Gaelic chief and of all the
red-handed crew he himself was the most terrible.

When he gave an order, a man obeyed instantly or
drew his weapon as swiftly. For the penalty of
disobedience or hesitancy was an instant dashing out of
the mutineer's brains beneath the savage chieftan's axe.
Men who had followed Turlogh O'Brien in the days
before his outlawry would have gaped at him now as he
stood on the bloodstained poop of *Crom's Hate*, eyes
blaxing and axe dripping, yelling commands to his motley
horde in a voice that was like the maddened yell of a
panther.

He was a pirate who preyed on pirates. Only when his
supplies were at ebb would he swoop down and harry the
fertile coasts of England, Wales or France. The almost
insane hatred for the Vikings that burned in his heart sent
him ravaging the strongholds of the raiders in the
Hebrides, the Orkneys and even on the coasts of the
Scandinavian mainlands. When driving sleet and winter
gales lashed the western seas, Turlogh and his tatter-
demalions rode the bitter wind, freezing, starving,
suffering, to fall on their foes with torch and sword.

It was a hard service the Gael offered the men who came to him from chains or the shadow of the gallows. He promised them only a hard, bitter life, ceaseless toil and warfare and a bloody death. But he gave them a chance to strike back at the world and to glut themselves in slaughter—and men followed him.

When even the stout Norsemen had their longships in the shiphouses and were pent in sturdy skallies, drinking ale and listening to the skalds, Turlogh and his thieves roamed the foaming wastes, to smite their enemies in their security and leave smoldering embers of strong steadings.

It was a day in deep winter. A bitter gale lashed the Baltic, driving before it a stinging sleet that froze on mast and rower's bench. Waves burst clear across the low waist of the dragon-ship, drenching the rowers and clotting their beards with ice. Even these men, inured to all hardships, who lived like wolves, were on the point of collapse. On the foredeck, with one hand on the arching prow that terminated in a dragon's head, Turlogh O'Brien strained his eyes, striving to pierce the veil of sleet and freezing spray.

There was ice on Turlogh's mail, and blood that caked his shoes was frozen stiff. But he gave no heed; at birth he had been flung into a snowdrift to decide his right to live. He was harder than a wolf. And now his heart burned in him so fiercely that no outer cold could harm him.

He had ventured far this voyage, and he had left smoldering ruins slaked in crimson, on the coasts of Jutland and the shores that hem the Skaggerack. Not content, he had swept on up into the Baltic and now believed he was in what was called by some the Gulf of Finland.

Suddenly he sighted a flying shape in the mist, and yelled fiercely. A longship! Some Viking farer who had put out to meet him, doubtless, having gotten wind of his

ravaging and not wishing to be caught napping in his
skalli, as had those sea-kings whose skulls now adorned
the shield-rail.

Turlogh, eyes fixed on that racing shadow, shouted a
command to alter the course and lay her alongside. His
Lieutenant, a grim, one-eyed Scotsman, dared an
objection.

"We've got to hold her in the wind; if we veer half a
point, a broadside sea will break her in two. It's mad
enough to venture among such seas in a ship with never a
deck to her—"

"The devil takes care of his own!" yelled Turlogh. "Do
as I say, you spawn of hell—there! She's faded into the
sleet—I can't see her—"

The huge ice-crested waves tossed the long, low craft
like a chip. The Scotsman was right; only a madman
would have ventured into those winter seas. But Turlogh
had a tinge of madness in his soul that broke its rein at
times.

Suddenly and without warning a beaked prow loomed
out of the driving mist on their port bow. The men of
Crom's Hate saw the horned helmets and the fierce blond
faces of the Norsemen who lined the rail, yelling and
brandishing their weapons.

"Run alongside and board her!" yelled Turlogh, as a
cloud of arrows whistled through the howling wind.
Crom's Hate leaped forward like a spurred horse, but an
instant later the strongest man at the sweep, a giant Saxon
with the brand of a runaway thrall on his face, dropped
with an arrow in his heart, and the kicking sweep head
resisted the efforts of his fellows. Turlogh yelled fiercely,
and others sprang forward, but the galley, out of control,
veered away, tossed and trembled to the impact of a
broadside sea that swept half a score men overboard, and
the Viking galley rammed her.

The iron beak of the Norsemen did not strike squarely, else it had sheared straight through the waist, but it ripped a great rent near her prow and scraped down the sides, with a deafening splintering of oars. The longships locked almost rail to rail, and the bulwarks were instantly thronged with howling, hacking figures that slew and died in a red holocaust of hate.

Men died like flies along the rails where axes shattered helm and skull, and swords broke in mailed bosoms. But the Scotch mate sought Turlogh where he slashed and hacked like a blood-hungry demon, and yelled: "The seas will tear us apart at any instant and *Crom's Hate* is sinking under our feet!"

"Lash them together!" yelled Turlogh, eyes ablaze and foam flecking his lips, his latent madness burst all bounds. "Lash them rail to rail and we'll drag these swine into Hell with us! We'll sink together and slay while we drown!"

And with his own hands he flung the first grappling hooks. The Vikings realized his intentions and sought to draw away, but too late. Locked together, there was no steering either ship. They were at the mercy of the winds and waves that tossed them and raced them dizzily along, while the crews closed in a last desperate grapple. Hacking and slashing in a red cataclysm of howling hell, Turlogh was vaguely aware that a great roaring ripped the din, like waves dashing on a rock-bound coast. But the berserk madness of slaying was on him and on all the rest and they ceased not to howl and ply their red axes as the two tortured ships, mastless, prowless and with splintered oars and timbers, hurled headlong through the surf to shatter on the foaming coast.

1

"AND you alone lived?" asked Somalkeld, breathlessly.

"I alone," answered Turlogh somberly. "Why, I know
not. In the midst of the tumult, darkness fell upon me and
I awaked in the hut of a strange people. Some whim of the
waves cast me ashore when all the rest died. But not alone
was I washed ashore. Many others the sea cast up, but
only I had a spark of life in me. The rest were slain of
wounds, water or cold. Many froze. I too, the people said,
was almost frozen. And my buckler and axe were gripped
in my hands so tightly they could not loosen them, and I
still gripped them so when I came to myself.

"Well, these folks were Finns—kindly people who
treated me well. With them I abode a space, but their land
was a barren one of ice and snow and when the time came
when I knew it was early spring in southern lands, I left
them. I had a horse of them, and I wandered south

through the great forests full of wolves and bears, and evil beasts whose shadows and footprints only I saw.

"I came upon fierce pagan tribes in these forests, some of which I fled from and some of which I tarried with. Some of these fold defied the grandsons of Rurik and I was well pleased to strike a blow against the Norsemen again. So I wandered for many months, first on the horse the Finns gave me, then on steeds I stole or bought, lastly on this great stallion that a pagan chief gave me. When I left the huts of the Finns it was late winter there. Now it is nearly winter again and I am still far from the southern lands my heart craves.".

"Come with me and dwell in the tents of my people, oh, my brother," urged Somakeld. "We are a brave people and we love warlike deeds. You shall be a chief. The girls of the Turgaslavs are fair. Dwell with my people."

Turlogh shrugged his shoulders. "I will ride with you, Somakeld, for my steed is weary and I am hungry. I will abide with you awhile because there is the smell of war in the land; aye, the ravens are gathering and I would not be put aside when the swords come to their quenching."

Night had fallen when the companions rode up to the encampment of the Turgaslavs. Turlogh had seen Tatar camps and this Slavic camp did not differ materially from them. The same high lumbering wagons, the same peaked saddles heaped carefully about, the same rings about the fires, where women cooked meat and passed about drinking horns of milk and mead. The Aryan and the Turanian nomad had progressed and evolved on much the same lines. Turlogh realized that he was gazing on a phase of Aryan life which was swift passing. The Aryan nomad was gradually quitting the pastoral life in favor of the agricultural life, or was being absorbed by the Tatar nomads.

Turlogh saw plenty of evidence that amalgamation was

already taking place among these ancient Aryan steppes lords and the Mongolian peoples. Many of the Turgaslavs had the broad faces and black hair that betokened a Tatar strain, and there was a fair sprinkling of pure-blood Tatars, though the bulk of the tribesmen were tall and big boned, with the light eyes and flaxen hair of the primitive Aryan. The admixture had already begun such as in later centuries was to produce the Cossacks.

The horses of these Aryan wanderers were tall and heavier than those ridden by the smaller Turks and Tatars, and their swords were long, straight and heavy, with both cutting edge and point. They were also armed with heavy axes, long spears and daggers, and bows, lighter and less effective than the bows of their Turanian rivals.

Their armor was crude and scanty, consisting largely of iron helmets, rude corselets of iron plates laced to heavy hide jackets, and round wooden, leather-covered and iron-braced bucklers. They wore as clothing, garments of sheepskin. The men were tall, upright in carriage and frank and open of countenance, while the women were pleasing in appearance.

Sentries on horseback roamed the steppe and these challenged the companions, but gave back at the word from Somakeld. A moon was rising as Turlogh and the youth trotted up the slope of the slight eminence whereon was pitched the Slavic camp, and sweeping the plains with his keen glance, Turlogh saw dark shadowy figures and lurching bulks cross the distant horizons, converging toward the camp on the rise.

"My people answer the call of war," said Somakeld, and the Gael nodded, his eyes glittering in the gloom as dim ancestral memories stirred vaguely in the sleeping deeps of his soul. Aye, the clans were gathering to feed the ravens as the Aryan clans had gathered in the dim lost ages—as the Gael's own ancestors had gathered on these very steppes, lurching along in clumsy wagons, or swinging on half-wild horses.

As they rode up to the fires a shout of welcome greeted them. Turlogh instantly picked out the chief—his name, as Somakeld had said, Hroghar Skel. He was old, but his long beard was still flaxen and when he rose to greet the stranger with simple stateliness, the Gael saw that he was mighty in stature and that age had not dimmed his eagle eye nor withered his iron muscles.

"Your face is new to me," said the chieftain in a deep calm voice. "You are neither Slav, Turk nor Tatar. But whoever you be, dismount and rest your steed. Eat and drink at our fires tonight."

"This is a noted warrior, oh *ataman*," exclaimed Somakeld. "A *bogatyr*, a hero! He has come to aid us against the Turks! By the honor of my clan, three Turks he sent to howl at the gates of Hell this day!"

The ancient inclined his lion-like head. "Our lives are yours, *bogatyr*."

As Turlogh swung from his saddle he noted another man squatted by the fire, a man in early middle life it seemed, with the broad, short build of the Tatar. This man had the bearing of a chief and beneath his sheepskins was the sheen of silks and the glimmer of silvered mail. His broad dark face was immobile, but his small beady eyes flickered as they rested on the splendid roan stallion. Behind the chief squatted a slim handsome youth, evidently his son. The Tatar's eyes rested long on the roan stallion.

Turlogh saw to his horse before he attended to his own needs, and assured that the roan was well cared for, he took a seat at the chieftain's fire. Somakeld, proud of his new acquaintance and of his own admission to the fire of the leaders, told the tale of his meeting with the Gael, and repeated the story of Turlogh's wanderings. All listened interestedly, and the new-comers, who were arriving in a steady stream, pressed close to gaze curiously at the Celt and to hear whispered versions of his exploits from folk of the outer rings.

"You have the look of an eagle, *bogatyr*," said Hroghar Skel. "Little matter to tell me you were a chief in your own land; well I know that you are a ruler of men. Well, the men of the Turgaslav need keen swords and strong wills. Khogar Khan moves against us and who knows how the war may go? The Turks are mighty fighters, and they have scattered like birds before the winds the warriors of Chaga Khan." And he nodded at the Tatar who sat drinking mare's milk.

"Aye," the Tatar's voice was like the rasp of a sword from its scabbard, "they were like wolves among sheep—by Erlik, they are madmen!"

"There is madness in them so that they fight as a stepped fire burns the grass," nodded Hroghar Skel. "There is magic in them that upholds them in the teeth of the spears. Khogar Khan claims descent from that red-handed scourge of old times, Attila the Hun. And more: he wears in his girdle the very sword which the Hun quenched in the blood of kings."

Turlogh gave a surprised exclamation.

The beady eyes of Chaga Khan turned on him.

"I saw it," the Tatar grunted, poising his drinking jack. "It was a red flame in his hand and with it he fed the kites. By Erlik, old Death ran before his steed and a black wind howled behind. When he smote it was as if a horde smote and no man could stand before him. He heaped my warriors in crimson ranks behind him to mark his course."

Silence reigned for a space. The night wind sighed through the high grass and the lurching rumble of distant wagons was heard, and the challenge of the outposts. Hroghar Skel shook his head and his iron hand was twisted in his beard.

"They gather fast; by dawn all the clans of the Turgaslav will be encamped and clamoring to be led against their enemies. But a cold doubt lies at the base of my brain. It is more than mortal men we fight."

All eyes turned toward Turlogh. Primitive people are swift to snatch at portents and supernatural conclusions. It seemed to them that Turlogh's coming was no chance thing, but that strange forces that work behind the veil had sent him to their aid. But the Gael merely said: "I will sleep."

As he stretched out on the sheepskins in Hroghar's tent, again deep ancestral feelings stirred in the Gael as he listened to the night sounds of the nomadic camp. All seemed friendly and familiar to him, the crackle of the fires, the scents of the cooking pots, the smell of sweaty leather and horseflesh, the jingle of bridles and the creak of saddles, the singing of the tribesmen and their laughter. These Slavs were of the very foundations of the Aryan race—the root and the stock. They clung close to that pristine existence that Turlogh's ancestors had abandoned so many centuries ago. Somakeld's people were fundamental, strong and clean with primal life and principle. They were knit close to the tie-ribs of existence, to the raw, red realities of life.

As he drifted into slumber, Turlogh's last vague waking thoughts were that though half a world lay between them and his people, the blood of these nomads was his own, and after centuries and wandering in alien lands, he had come home at last. Then he sank into sleep haunted by dreams wherein he, light-eyed, wild, skin-clad, traversed endless leagues of forest and plain in lurching, oxen-pulled wagons, or on the backs of half-wild horses, and in company of his wild, light-eyed, skin-clad kind, roared and slashed in nameless battles in dim, lost lands, fought man and beast and foaming torrents, and trampled tottering civilizations that were old when the world was young—so in his dreams he wandered and fought again down dim, lost ages.

2

HROGHAR SWEPT his hand around in a gesture that took in all the camp, where women cooked food and mended harness and men whetted swords.

"These are all my people. I can muster but seven hundred warriors, strong able men, neither too young nor too old to fight. Some three hundred Tatars hunt with us; they will fight for us as long as the arrows fly, but we cannot depend upon them to stand when it comes to sword strokes. Khogar Khan has a good thousand riders, and five hundred Tatar allies."

"What of Chaga Khan?" demanded Turlogh.

Hroghar shook his head.

"The Tatars are like wolves that make a ring about two warring bulls, to devour the loser. Chaga Khan sent to us to ask for aid, but joined battle before we could come to his help. He feels he owes us nothing. His people have withdrawn far to the east. He waits to see how we will stand up against the Turks. These Tatars who cleave to us, and they whom Khogar Khan has impressed into his service are of small roving clans. Chaga Khan's tribe is the most powerful one in this part of the steppes. Despite his defeat by the Turks, he can still muster a thousand riders."

"Then in the name of the Devil," snapped Turlogh, "can you not make him understand that if he joined forces with you, you would defeat the Turks?"

The old Slav shrugged his shoulders. "Little use to argue with a Tatar. Khogar Khan struck fear into him and he is afraid to go up against the Turk. And I am not so sure that he wishes to aid me, anyway. He will watch which way the feather falls. If we win, he will come back to his old pasture lands. If the Turk wins, he may retire further into the East, even into the deserts of his people, or he may join forces with Khogar Khan. He believes that the Turk will be a great conqueror, like Attila his ancestor, and it is good to follow the banners of a conqueror."

"Then why not ally yourself to Khogar Khan?" Turlogh watched the old chief's face narrowly. The mighty hand on the spear-shaft shook with anger; Hroghar's eyes blazed.

"We white-skins have been lords of the steppes for untold ages. Hence went conquering hordes to people the world. When we were many we lashed the dark-faced people back into the Eastern deserts. Now that we are weak and few, we make them the same reply our ancestors made: 'Death to you, dog-brothers!' Our fair Lord God made us the masters of all other races. If I treat with these Moslem jackals for peace, may the heart rot in my bosom!" Turlogh grinned hardly and bleakly. "There is iron in you, old man! But you have overlooked one thing: even if we win, the tribe will be greatly weakened, and

Chaga Khan and his jackals may swoop down and wipe out what is left of us."

Hroghar plucked his beard. "True; but what can we do?"

The Gael shrugged his shoulders. "How will you fight these Turks?"

"Why, lord sir, in the same manner we always fight; we will mount our steeds and gallop across the steppes until we meet their horde and then we will shout our war-cry and charge in and cut them down like grain."

"And will they not bend their bows and shoot you out of your saddles before you can come to grips?" Turlogh growled.

"There will be a flight of arrows," agreed the Turgaslav. "But these Turks are not like the Tatars; they like sword strokes. They will loose a cloud of shafts as they charge and then rush in with naked steel. Chaga Khan's warriors had the better of it as long as the battle was an exchange of arrows, but when the Turks rode in among them, they could not stand before them. The Moslems are bigger men and better armed."

"Good," grunted Turlogh. "You are bigger men than the Turks and will have the same advantage with them that they had with the Tatars. But the Turgaslavs must come swiftly to exchange of sword strokes if they are to win."